Sign up for our newsletter to hear about new and upcoming releases.

www.ylva-publishing.com

Bunny
FINDS A
FRIEND

Hazel Yeats

To Kasja
Inspirator. Motivator.

Chapter 1

CARA KNEW THAT SOMETHING WAS off, but it took her a second to realize what it was. The *ho ho ho* sure was jolly enough, but it lacked Santa's characteristic baritone. It was more of a soprano, angelic enough to land him the lead in an all-girls choir. As Cara approached the throne on which he was sitting, she realized that this wasn't the only thing about him that was different. He seemed a little girly. He seemed to wear a little rouge on his cheeks. He seemed unable to hide the fact that, under his clearly fake pot belly, he was quite slender and elegant.

She sighed. Just her luck. Had she not decided that the road to celibacy was the only one for her—the only *right* one? And was it not a little ironic that fate chose to practically throw this gorgeous Kristina Kringle in her lap only hours later? Then again, maybe it was the ultimate test. A chance to prove that she stood by her resolution. Because if she was able to resist a saint, a hot saint at that, then surely she would be rewarded by losing her sex drive and become a crocheting spinster in flannel slippers.

Doing a survey of the women she'd been involved with over the last decade had made her realize that most of them had been either narcissistic, unfaithful, emotionally confused, or teetering on the brink of an alcohol addiction. In some cases, with a considerable overlap. She'd had a call from Kelly, her girlfriend of two months, that very morning. Kelly told her, in a tearful voice, that she was going off to find herself—not in an ashram or sweat hut, as Cara had always thought she one day would, but in the arms of a straight co-worker. Or formerly straight. Or fluently straight. Or whatever.

Cara hadn't presumed that she and Kelly were meant to last, but it stung anyway. When she'd hung up the phone, she had somehow understood that every relationship she would ever have would be doomed. Call it kismet, call it karma, call it bad luck, but the coupling thing wasn't for her. And since all her coupling had started by noticing a woman's angelic voice and slender elegance, she vowed to close her eyes as she handed Santa the papers.

Now, all she needed was to find a way to do so inconspicuously, which wouldn't be easy given the fact that she was on the ground floor of De Bijenkorf and that it was one of the busiest days of the year. The luxury, upmarket department store, centrally located at Dam Square in the heart of Amsterdam, was a magnet for both locals and tourists, especially around Christmas. The striking, historic building appealed to people—its spectacular façade lighting, the extravagant window displays, the large light dome, and six floors of luxury goods. Outside the store, in the square, there was a Christmas tree soaring over twenty meters into the Amsterdam sky, decorated by four kilometers of Christmas lights.

Even Cara mellowed at the sight of so much beauty. But then she remembered that she had a job to do, and she hurried inside.

Santa's little enclave, prominently situated among the shop-in-shops of high-end fashion brands, was enclosed by a wooden fence with a gate at the front—now open to let the children in. There were two huge Christmas trees on either side of Santa's throne, decorated in gold and red. Scattered around the compound were three remarkably lifelike reindeer, their antlers as large as tree branches. Two children, dressed as elves, were busy moving gift-wrapped boxes from one place to the other. The floor was covered with snow blankets. From the speakers came the sound of Christmas carols.

Cara took off her gloves and unzipped her coat. It was unseasonably warm today, and there were far too many people here. About a thousand more than she was comfortable with. She lingered at a safe distance from Santa's chair, holding on to the railing to avoid getting trampled by the crowd, and watched him, or rather her, operate for a moment. Santa seemed very comfortable in her role, despite the gender confusion. She had an electric sort of energy. She was bouncing up and down, laughing, and spreading joy. She looked as natural in her red and white getup as though she wore nothing else all year round. The children were lined up waiting to take their places on her lap, eager to tell her what they were expecting to find under the tree in three weeks' time.

Cara watched the line grow and panicked. Was she going to stand here all day, waiting for a lull in Santa's schedule, to hand her the envelope? Cara was new at this—in fact, Santa was her first client. She'd had instructions, sure, an official training even. She had diligently read the entire manual, but there hadn't been anything in the rules about how to act when your first client happened to be Father Christmas. Let alone *Mother* Christmas.

She braced herself, pushing her elbows forward in the hope of lending her girly features a little brazenness, and cut in front of the waiting children.

"Hey!" a stout boy in a blue anorak shouted. "Wait your turn."

Cara turned and crouched down, facing him. "Now look, you little twerp," she said, pointing a finger at him. "I'm not having a very good day here. Me and Santa have some business, okay? So just back off and give me a moment."

The boy, startled by her aggressive tone, stepped back, almost knocking over the kid who was in line behind him, who promptly started to bawl.

Cara walked through the gate as soon as Santa's lap was empty. She took a few steps, until she was close enough to get Santa's attention. The chair was quite high, and she had to look up.

"Hi," Santa said. "I appreciate your eagerness to sit on my lap, but would you mind terribly *not* scaring away the customers? This is a once-a-year gig, as you may know, so it's important I keep them happy."

Cara stared at the woman, her mouth dropping. She had some nerve!

"So, what can I do for you?" Santa looked at the envelope in Cara's hand. "Is that your list?"

Cara shook her head.

"In that case, just *tell* me what you want." She eyed Cara critically, then pointed what Cara knew to be a mocking finger at her official process server badge. "I'd suggest a shiny ornament for your lapel, but I see that's been taken care of."

"I'm good," Cara said. She sighed. "That was funny, by the way."

Santa flashed her an innocent smile. "Then perhaps someone to pull the stick out of your ass?"

Cara threw the woman an angry look and resisted, with some difficulty, the temptation to climb on the chair and smack her in the face. There was to be no physical contact, let alone violence. Not only was she here in an official capacity, but this was one Santa you didn't want to get into a fight with.

She gave Santa a cold look. "Strong language coming from someone in your position."

Santa smiled again. Cara noticed her perfect, white teeth. She also noticed her gorgeous, hazel eyes. Most of the rest of her face was not visible through the beard. It was funny, Cara mused, how she could see so little of Santa's face and still somehow know that she was quite attractive. It made her want to rip the beard off to see the rest of her. She kicked herself, mentally, and pushed all thoughts of Santa's physical appeal to the back of her mind. She cursed herself for even noticing these completely irrelevant details about someone who was obviously an asshole.

"I don't know what it is," Santa said, "some people just bring that out in me."

Cara was beginning to be very aware of how she was holding up the line. It was time to wrap this up or all hell would break loose. And besides, there was no reasoning with this woman. She could stand here and argue with her all day and accomplish nothing.

"Whatever," she said, as "O Holy Night" wafted from the shop speakers. "Are you Jude Donovan?"

"Shush!" said Santa. She pressed a finger to her lips, then pointed to the waiting children. "Don't say that out loud."

Cara followed her gaze. Yes, there were children, so what? She turned back and waited for an answer, that didn't come.

"Well?" She was getting impatient. "Are you?"

Santa shook her head. "No, I'm Kris."

Cara stared at the envelope, once again reading the name.

"Kris Kringle!" the woman said, seeing Cara's confusion. "*You* know. Santa?"

"Seriously." Cara heard the voices of protesting parents and felt a bead of sweat begin to trickle down her back. "I really need you to confirm that you're Jude Donovan."

"Okay," Santa said. "Not that it's any of your business, but yes, I'm…" her voice became a whisper, as she leaned over to where Cara was standing "…I'm her. I'm Jude Donovan."

Cara nodded and handed Santa the envelope, which she took with a bewildered expression.

Cara curtsied. "You have been served."

༄ ༄ ༄

"A guy?" Inge opened the Styrofoam box with eager fingers. "How could you think someone named Jude is a guy?"

Cara shrugged. "I just assumed. Aren't all Judes guys? *Jude the Obscure*? Jude Law? The dude in Hey Jude?"

"Not sure about *Jude the Obscure*. I guess when you're obscure you have more important things to worry about than your gender."

Cara looked at her sister critically. "Do you even know what obscure means?"

"Sure," Inge said. "Invisible, right?"

6

Cara nodded. "Right. Thomas Hardy spent many a sleepless night wondering if he shouldn't have called his novel *Jude the Invisible*."

"There's no need to go all literary and intellectual on me." Inge crumbled up a napkin and threw it at Cara. "After all, you don't even know what sex the average Jude is."

"Most of them are men." Cara bent over to pick up the napkin from the floor and put in on her tray.

"Anyway," Inge said, "tell me more about the lovely Santa." She sank her teeth into her double cheeseburger and moaned. Cara watched her like a mother watches a child enjoying an unhealthy but much deserved treat; with that curious combination of guilt and satisfaction. She was the only person in Inge's circle of friends and family who didn't point blank refuse to eat at a McDonald's, even though she hadn't personally felt the desire to set foot in one since the age of twelve. She didn't care for the menu, or the garish, plastic ambiance, but she didn't have the problem with fast food that Myra and Alice had. Cara felt strongly that adults should decide for themselves what they did, or did not, want to eat. With Myra busy doing whatever it is that mothers of large families do during the day, and Alice in Milan to discuss the deeper meaning of below-the-knee hemlines, Cara had decided to indulge her beloved sibling. After all, hadn't Inge willingly accompanied her to gay bars and Pink concerts through the years, without being particularly passionate about either? Watching her devour a Happy Meal every now and then was the least she could do to pay Inge back for her support.

"I wouldn't call her lovely." Cara shook her head. "And besides, I make it a rule not to look at the people I serve in that way."

"You do, huh? So far you've told me about the length of her lashes, the swell of her breasts under the grubby Santa suit, and how her smile seems like the sun coming out after a long and harsh winter. How is that not *that* way?"

Cara frowned. "I'm positive I never said a word about any swell."

"It was implied," said Inge. "So what happens next?"

"With her, you mean? I don't know. It's got nothing to do with me. I just deliver the paperwork and that's it."

"So you haven't been back to the store to see whether she's still there?"

"Of course not."

"Want to go down there?" Inge held the red container upside down. The last two crunchy french fries fell into her hand.

"What?" Cara said. "Now? Why?"

"To see if she's kept her job, of course." Inge looked to her left and right before eyeing Cara. "What if," she whispered, bringing her face closer to her sister's, "she has to stand trial for a horrible crime? Like murder."

"Yes," Cara said. She sighed. "That's very likely. Don't you think they'll be checking the credentials of a person who applies for a job at a public place? A person who'll be working with children?"

Inge shrugged. "I'm not saying she's necessarily the one who committed the murder, am I? Maybe she was simply an innocent witness. Someone who happened to be at the wrong place at the wrong time. Like at a horrible crime scene, where she stumbled upon a barely breathing victim, lying broken in a pool of blood."

"Ugh," Cara said. "That's gross." She saw Inge eye her own french fry cup. "Aren't you getting a little carried away here?"

"I'm just curious." Inge reached over the table for the red container and held it up. "Are you eating these?"

Cara shook her head. "Be my guest."

Inge emptied the box on the tray. "All I'm saying is that I'd want to know what's going on with her if I were you. You're obviously intrigued."

"What if she's not there? And I'll be forever wondering?"

Inge shrugged. "Then I guess we owe it to her to find out what happened. It's not unthinkable that she's in the witness protection program."

"Is that not, by its nature, something we're unlikely to discover?"

"It may be for mere mortals, but you're a government official with access to classified information, right?"

Cara shook her head. "Far from it. If anything, I'm a glorified mailman."

"Anyway," Inge insisted. "I just want to see Hot Santa."

Cara looked at her sister in horror. "Please," she moaned, "tell me you're not going through some weird bi-curious phase. Because I really can't deal with that right now."

"Spare me," said Inge. "I find it beyond imagining how you people can go through life never feeling a—"

"Whoa!" said Cara. "Please don't finish that."

"Don't have to." Inge giggled. "You know exactly what I mean. So, are you coming? If you do, I'll spring for lunch."

Cara shook her head. "It was your turn anyway. So I think I'll pass. I have work to do. Those legal documents aren't going to deliver themselves."

Inge responded by stuffing the very last fries in her mouth.

꙳ ꙳ ꙳

Three days later, Cara's curiosity got the better of her. She took an irresponsible detour between assignments, which basically meant that she was playing hooky, so there was no time to waste. She checked her watch, sighing as she realized that she was supposed to be in a housing project in Almere, trying to serve debt collection papers to the same guy for the fourth time. Every time she rang his doorbell, a dog started to bark, or rather whimper—not aggressively, more like hopelessly. She tried not to think about the possibility that her client had vacated the premises, leaving the poor animal behind. After she had failed to find him home, twice, she brought huge amounts of dog treats and kibble the third time. She dropped the food through the mailbox in hopes the dog would find it, and praying that she wasn't just prolonging his agony. The realization that she couldn't get him any water kept her up at night, which is why she made an extra trip there and rang the neighbor's doorbell. A middle-aged man answered the door—drowsy, or drunk, and smelling of old sweat. He assured Cara that the dog's owner came home regularly, walked the dog on those occasions, and left enough food and water for the animal when he 'went on business.' He also promised her to keep an eye on things.

As Cara walked through the revolving door into De Bijenkorf, she looked to her left and right, trying to be inconspicuous, as if she were about to engage in some criminal act. The thought that only minutes from now she would be face to face with the woman who'd been on her mind constantly these past days, for no apparent reason, made her heart beat in her chest.

The feeling of total disappointment when she saw, at first glance, that sexy Santa was no longer there, was so overwhelming that, for a second, her whole world went black.

The scene was exactly as it had been before. The trees were there, the elves, the kids, Vixen, Blitzen, Cupid, and, most importantly, Santa's throne.

What was clearly very different, was the person sitting on the throne. Santa's pot belly was real, and so was his deep voice. Jude Donovan was gone.

Chapter 2

ON FRIDAY, AT TWO P.M. on the dot, they met up for lunch at Inge's. As always, she served tons of food: sandwiches, olives, fish, meatballs, pickles, cheeses, and cold cuts.

Alice swallowed a piece of smoked salmon and grinned. "You curtsied?"

Cara nodded. "I did."

"And you actually said, 'you're being served?'" Alice was trying hard not to laugh. "Wasn't that a little...dramatic?"

Cara reached for her glass and frowned. "I wanted to lend a bit of class to the whole thing, okay? She was quite rude. And she was my first one." Cara paused. "Also, I've always wanted to say that."

The front door swung open. Bart wandered in from the street, where he was working on his car, and put a bottle of Turtle Wax on the dinner table.

"What have you always wanted to say, Sis?" He wiped his hand on an oil soaked rag. Cara smiled at her brother-in-law. Her dependable, good-natured brother-in-law. She shook her head. "Never mind. Not for you."

"Honey," Inge said, "could you not put your greasy car stuff on my table?"

Bart shrugged. "Is this one of those occasions where men are supposed to make themselves scarce?" He picked up the wax and eyed his wife suspiciously. "Or did you ladies honor our home with your presence because you want the male perspective on your troubles?"

"If you must know," Myra said, "we're honoring your home with our presence because once a week it's Sister Day at *Casa Inge*. And this week, it happens to be today." She smiled at Alice. "I mean, of course, Sister *and* Sister-in-law Day."

"Yes." Alice sighed. "I know I owe my place in your sister posse to Arend."

"If Arend and I ever split up," Myra said, "heaven forbid, then we will keep you on as a member of the family, I promise. We'll adopt you as our own sister. I'm sure my parents would love to have another daughter. We never give them any trouble, and never have."

"So basically you're banning me from my own house?" Bart said.

"That's right, honey." Inge dipped a meatball in mustard.

"Which isn't to say that we wouldn't appreciate your input," Alice said.

"You're just being polite, aren't you?" He smiled.

Inge nodded. "We are."

"I see," he said. "I will make myself scarce, then. But if you should change your mind, I'll be in the back yard. Holler if you need me, okay?"

"So, why a department store?" Alice asked, as soon as Bart had closed the door behind him. "Why couldn't you have delivered the papers to her house?"

"I actually thought that was a little weird myself," Cara said. "But my instructions were clear. I guess that maybe they had tried her house and she was never there. We deliver documents to the weirdest places."

"Poor you," Inge said with an evil grin. "You were so close to finding out where she lives."

"Shut up, okay?" said Cara.

"So why did you quit?" Alice asked.

Cara shrugged. "The thrill wore off."

"After two weeks?"

Cara couldn't recall a time when she wasn't expected to explain her every action to her much older sisters. And after Myra married Arend and they all became friends with Alice, she joined the pack, so then there were three to gang up on her. It wasn't always easy being the baby of the family. Her sisters seemed to regard her as an improved version of themselves, someone who wasn't allowed to make mistakes or to go through phases of doing stupid things. Mothering her was second nature to them. And though Cara was, on occasion, quite happy to turn to them when she needed someone to talk to, she didn't care for the way her chosen path in life (or her inability to choose a path in life) tended to be criticized. They expected her to make nothing but sensible choices and grown-up decisions. They expected her to be responsible. To commit. And she wasn't ready to commit. Not to a job, not to a woman. She knew she would always get edgy when her time wasn't her own to squander. She needed a bit of breathing space, and she didn't think there was anything wrong with a little job hopping or even a little girlfriend hopping. She was thirty-two, what did they expect? Wasn't she supposed to try things out before she settled on anything permanently? Then again, she may never commit. Maybe she was just that kind of person—restless, adventurous.

"The thing is," she said, "I didn't have a clear picture of what the job was all about. I thought I was going to be like this really cool private eye, hunting down criminals, driving my convertible along the coastline, the scent of the sea my only company." She bowed her head. "Instead, I kept finding myself on the doorsteps of shabby family homes, serving my papers to tired housewives whose asshole husbands' cars were being repossessed."

"So?" said Myra. "Doesn't every job have its downside?"

Cara shrugged. "It was depressing, not to mention that the pay doesn't become interesting until you get a case that poses a serious threat to your safety."

"So basically, you thought you were going to move to California and be Kinsey Millhone."

"Who?"

"Kinsey Millhone," Inge said. "Beloved private eye in Sue Grafton's alphabet series of thrillers!"

They all drew a blank.

"Jesus," she said finally. "What's wrong with you people? Would it kill you to pick up a book once in a while?"

"Sorry," Cara said. "Perhaps you should give us some reading advice." She pushed her sister playfully. "I hear you're quite the expert on *Jude the Invisible*."

"I can hardly find the time to breathe," Myra said. "Let alone pick up a book." She rested the palm of her hand lovingly on her stomach, currently home to her fourth child. Cara and Alice were sitting next to her on the couch, fighting for the available space.

"Anyway," she said, turning to Cara. "I guess what we're trying to say is that we're a little worried about you. I thought that with Kelly in your life and the new job..."

Her voice trailed off, and Cara could just tell that her oldest sister was picturing her wheeling a pram down the street, or giving a closing argument in a courtroom.

"Kelly has found solace in the arms of another," she said. "who brings light to her life where I brought nothing but darkness."

"Really?" said Myra. "What a horrible thing to do. And you two seemed so content together. Like two kittens."

"It's fine," Cara said. "The kitten left some nasty scratches, but they've healed and now I'm perfectly okay. There's absolutely no need to worry about me."

"It's just that you don't seem to be...going anywhere," Myra insisted.

"Nobody's going anywhere," Cara said. "Where we're all going, is to our graves. What's important is that we have a bit of fun until that day arrives."

"So are you?" Alice asked.

"Am I what?"

"Having fun."

"Sure." Cara nodded, as Inge pointed to her empty wine glass—yes, she wanted a refill. Being interrogated like this was always easier with a little alcohol to take the edge off.

"Sure, I'm having fun," she said. "No more or less than any one of you."

Inge filled the wine glasses and teacups. When she helped herself to a big wedge of cheese her sisters started screaming, keeping their promise to help her lose weight.

"Oh, shut up," she said. "Bart told me, only yesterday, that he likes a bit of meat on me." She looked smug. "There's more of me to love."

Alice ran her hands over her hips, as if to make sure they were still as slim as she needed them to be.

"If you ask me," Cara continued, "this whole concept of going somewhere is a typically unenlightened, western-culture way to deal with mortality. Or rather, to *not* deal with it. To try and push it away. Instead, we have to embrace it. Because it keeps us on our toes. And because it won't be ignored. There's no such thing as being in control of your life; no matter how big your house, or how steady your job, or how healthy your diet. It ends when it does. A blood clot, a car crash, a nuclear disaster—*something* will be our undoing. We have no say in the matter."

"You're overthinking things," said Myra. "We're talking about instinct here. It's very natural to have goals in your life. To want a family. A home. Maybe you'll even want a home here—in the suburbs. Or at least in a better part of the city, with fewer gunfights and muggings. You need some security."

"Security makes me feel as though somebody is sitting on my chest, making it impossible for me to breathe," said Cara. "And I'll have you know that I've never been mugged or shot. I simply can't afford to spend 4,000 euros a month on a studio apartment, and I'm not ready to live the life of a Stepford wife in some ghost town that was reclaimed from the sea no more than a couple of decades ago."

"We're all different, I guess," remarked Alice. "I, for one, find an incredible sense of security in the thought that I'll be picking up my new car later today." She looked at her Rolex. "In less than three hours, to be exact."

"Finding your sense of security in possessions isn't healthy either, if you ask me." Myra cast Alice a disapproving look. "You and Arend are so different that way."

"Arend used to be like me." Alice said. "But then you guys had all those kids and he had no choice but to shift his priorities."

"I find my sense of security in food," Inge confessed. It was something that she had obviously made her peace with.

"Let's just say," Cara concluded, "that we're all dealing with life's issues in unhealthy ways, okay? I'm too flaky, Inge eats too much, Alice spends too much, and Myra has too much unprotected sex. So what? I say we're all just fine the way we are, and I for one love you guys no matter what."

"Hear hear," said Myra, before she gulped down the last of her tea.

"So anyway," Inge said, wiping the bread crumbs off her shirt, "remember this Santa woman we were talking about? Our Cara's got a thing for her."

☽ ☾ ☾

"I do *not* have a thing for her," Cara said to herself as she drove home. "Far from it. She was obnoxious, she was hostile, and I wouldn't be surprised if she had to stand trial for killing off the Easter bunny."

She knew that her words were hollow. If she couldn't even believe them herself, how would she convince someone else? Okay, the woman *had* been obnoxious, but she was also funny, and pretty gorgeous from what little the Santa suit had revealed of her. And the truth was that Cara hadn't exactly been a ray of sunshine herself that day.

What if Jude had been fired because of her? Had Cara not totally disrupted the peace, yelling at the boy and arguing with Santa? Kids had started crying, parents had given her angry looks. What if Jude had lost her job because of it, through no fault of her own? She had been so good at what she did. And what if the performance she had referred to as her once-a-year gig was her *only* gig? What if playing

Santa was like her career, and her sole source of income? As her heart swelled with compassion at the thought that Jude Donovan might be penniless, Cara suddenly realized that her own circumstances weren't any less dire. The process server position wasn't at all what she'd expected. It was supposed to be a fast-paced job, exciting and dangerous, and she was looking forward to the thrill it would bring. But it didn't. At all. She served people who didn't want to be served, who were often aggressive and frequently desperate—it was the opposite of what she'd thought it would be. She wasn't cut out for it. She gave it a chance, hoping it would grow on her, but when it started keeping her up at night she decided to quit, having lasted less than two weeks. She handed in her badge and went home with her last pay check. She'd have to find a new job, but since nobody was hiring staff so close to Christmas, she decided to take a couple of weeks off and not look for employment until the new year. She supposed she could devote her time to trying to find Jude Donovan, but she wasn't sure where else to look for her except at the store where she'd found her. She parked her car and walked home, pulling her scarf up to her ears. It was probably time to leave the incident behind her.

The next time she caved and went to De Bijenkorf to try and find Jude, she was shocked to find that the previously live Christmas show had been turned into a set of props. The elves were gone, and so was Santa. The packages lay motionless under the trees. The reindeer were there, but the absence of people in the enclave made them look every bit as lifeless as they were.

Cara swore under her breath. Somewhere in the universe, someone, or something, was doing everything in their power to keep her and Jude apart. It seemed that Jude was drifting further away from her with each passing day.

As she stood there feeling bleak, her eye suddenly caught a person in a Santa suit going up the escalator. She would have to move fast. She ran across the store, past the Louis Vuitton, Hermès, Burberry, and Gucci shops. She excused herself to everybody she almost knocked down in the process. She stepped on the escalator, walking up the moving steps to try and catch up with Santa, who was kind enough to stand still, so that she was gaining on him. They stepped off the escalator at the same time. Santa hurried away, but Cara followed him—or, as she was feverishly hoping, *her*—and as she came up from behind, she tapped Santa on the shoulder.

"Excuse me." She leaned forward to catch a glimpse of Santa's face.

As soon as Santa turned, Cara's heart sank. This was most definitely a guy. And not exactly the sort of guy that was a credit to his gender, either. He was scrawny, kept pulling at his beard, and had bloodshot eyes.

His head shot up. "What?"

"I'm very sorry," Cara said. "But I was actually looking for a colleague of yours. Do you work on the ground floor?"

A store customer, with her arms full of bags, elbowed Cara out of the way to get to the escalator. Cara almost lost her balance.

"Do I what?" Santa snorted. He eyed her suspiciously. "Don't tell me you're with the Tax Office!"

Cara shook her head. "I just need some information. Do you know who else has been playing Santa here at the store?"

I sound like an idiot, she thought. A desperate, lovesick idiot.

Santa shook his head. "How the fuck should I know who does what here, lady? What do you think I am, a fucking information board? Don't you think I have better things to do with my time?"

"I thought you might belong to some kind of collective," Cara explained. "You know, working in a group, taking turns."

"Some kind of collective?" Angry Santa scratched his cheek. "What are you, nuts?"

"I'm probably mistaken." Cara was beginning to fear he would smack her, which is why she smiled amiably. She hated him, but he might be her very last link to Jude.

"Would you mind telling me who hires you?" she asked.

"Queen Maxima hired me, okay? She called me up herself."

"I see," Cara said. She sighed.

Santa belched. "You know what? Maybe we should discuss this later." He looked Cara up and down and it was clear from his smirk that he liked what he saw. "I'm a little pressed for time right now, but my evening happens to be wide open. So how about sharing a little...you know... eggnog later. Just you and me, okay?"

Cara looked at him with a face full of loathing. Then she turned around and stepped back on the escalator.

Going down.

ↄ ☽ ↄ

Christmas came and went. Cara drove to her mother's house, in a blizzard, on Christmas Eve and spent two seemingly endless days trying to pacify her expanding family. Even Myra and Arend were arguing, and Inge, the great peacemaker, unfortunately wasn't there to help her bring any festiveness to the mood. She was glad when it was finally over.

She spent New Year's Eve with Inge and Bart, who had invited a lot of people, most of whom were strangers to her. She sat next to a guy with a moustache and a passion for model trains. He talked too much, and he smelled funny. Not necessarily bad, but funny. Like cotton candy. After his third beer, he moved closer and put his hand on her knee, the alcohol giving him the courage to make a pass at her. She protested only lightly when he planted his lips on hers at midnight.

She was beginning to forget about Jude Donovan.

Chapter 3

IN THE SECOND HALF OF January, she found a job delivering pizzas. Alice called it an all-time low, but Cara had found the ATM machine empty, and she was in dire need of some cash.

For some reason, she liked her new position, humble though it may be. It felt good, after the process server job, to have people actually be glad to see her when she rang their doorbells. In a nation, as tiny as the Netherlands was, that ordered five thousand take-out meals a day, her future at Cara Mia was quite secure. What she did was so much more than simply deliver food. Not everybody would greet her wallet in hand and slam the door in her face. Many of her customers had to find money first—rummaging through pockets, looking for purses. Cara waited patiently, watching their kids stare at her, listening to their dogs bark at her, smelling their smells, stealing looks at their interiors, gracefully accepting their tips, and being appalled at the filthy rags some people were comfortable answering the door in.

There were definitely people who couldn't get rid of her fast enough, but some struck up conversations, even confided in her. Many excused themselves for the state of their apartments, although generally not the ones who had the most reason to. Some didn't credit her with so much as a look, but quite a few made a pass at her. All men, never women. Some subtle, some not so subtle. Some were grown men, whose wives she could see setting the table in the background. But mostly it was young men—students with an attitude, whose expression would change dramatically the minute they laid eyes on her; or teenage boys, clumsy and sweaty, always knocking things over or dropping their change.

There were horrible ones too—condescending ones, rude ones, drunk ones, dirty ones, broke ones.

The pay was moderate, but the tips made up for a lot.

Delivering pizzas was so much more than handing over a grease-stained cardboard box—it was a study of the human condition.

୨ ଓ ୨

"Another day, another lunch." Inge rubbed her hands together.

It was Friday. Alice was the only one who was supposed to go back to work. For the other three, there was no curfew today.

They were at their favorite deli, a little restaurant in Amsterdam's Nine Streets district—a collection of narrow passages which traverse the city's canals. It was an elegant place, with original wooden paneling, upholstered walls, and oak flooring. Inge liked to say that the food was almost as good as hers.

"Wonderful." Alice leafed through the menu, although she knew it by heart. "I'm starving. I think I'll have the small goat cheese salad."

Inge snorted. "That's what you have when you're starving? So what do you have when you're just a little hungry?"

"A glass of water," Alice said.

Inge stuck out her tongue to Alice, then turned to Cara. "So how are you, baby Sis? How's the search for Jude?"

Myra, who had been busy trying to remove a stain from her collar with a wet napkin, was now all ears. Her eyes grew wide. "Jude? Who's Jude?"

"Nobody," Cara said. "The search is off."

"Jude Donovan," Inge explained. "Also known as Hot Santa."

Myra had never looked more surprised. "Jude Donovan?"

Inge nodded. "Do you know her?"

"Not *the* Jude Donovan?"

Oh God, Cara thought. I was right. It was on the news. She killed herself. She was found in an alley, starved to death. Cara had long since abandoned the thought that there might have been anything incriminating in the documents she had delivered to the woman. If this was never going to be more than a fantasy, then she might as well make it a good one, where Jude was a hot saint rather than a hot criminal. Her feelings had gone through this weird transition since that fateful day at the store, from angry and offended to caring and compassionate. Their encounter was like a fan fiction story now, where the actual event had been rewritten into something it never was, and was never supposed to become. It was taking on a life of its own.

"What do you mean, *the* Jude Donovan?" asked Inge.

"Duh!" Myra said. "The famous American children's book writer." She stared at three pairs of raised eyebrows. "The Bunny series. Seriously?"

"I am now officially an illiterate," Alice complained. "First Kinsey Millhone, and now a Bunny whose fame has apparently eluded me."

"*Bunny Goes on a Trip. Bunny Has a Baby Sister.*" Myra shook her head at their ignorance. "It's literature for toddlers! It deals with life's issues in a way they will understand and respond to." She was looking as proud as if Bunny were her own creation. "The twins' absolute favorite is *Bunny Has a Boo-Boo.*"

Inge burst out laughing. "They should totally make a grown-up version!" She hollered. "*Bunny Has a Really Bad Hangover.*"

Alice smirked. "*Bunny Fakes an Orgasm.*"

"Thank you guys," Myra said, casting them an angry look, "for ruining that for me. I will never look at Bunny the same way again."

Cara still hadn't spoken. She was dumbfounded.

"But is this Jude the same person as Cara's Jude?" Inge asked.

"We can find that out right now." Myra picked her giant purse off the floor, groping about inside. "If I'm not mistaken, I happen to have here…" To everybody's surprise, she presented a children's book with a giant, white rabbit on the cover. "Ta-dah."

"You carry those with you even when the kids aren't around?" Alice looked at the book in disgust.

"Sure," Myra said. "Being a mom isn't like a nine-to-five job, you know. It's a round-the-clock commitment." She pointed to the purse. "I'm sure I have a bib in there somewhere. And a pacifier. And a stuffed giraffe."

"Honestly." Alice stole a look at her own Birkin bag. "I don't know how you can live like that."

"Gimme." Inge yanked the book from Myra's hand. She turned it over and found what she was looking for. A picture of the author.

"Wow," she said. "She *is* hot."

Cara was afraid to look. She wanted to think of Jude only in private, not share her like this. But her eyes strayed, and before she knew it, Inge was pushing the book in her face.

"Is it her?' she said. "Was Santa quite so…Mediterranean looking?"

Cara stared at the picture, realizing that it was impossible to tell, without the Santa outfit, if the dark-haired, olive-skinned woman in the picture was the one she'd been arguing with all those weeks ago. Whether she was or not, there was every reason to keep staring at her photo as long as she could. Cara smirked. Maybe she should ask Myra if she could take the book home. After all, what better way to go off to dreamland than reading a good story?

"What's that look?" Inge asked suspiciously. "It's her, isn't it?"

Cara shook her head. "I honestly don't know," she said, handing the book back to Myra.

"You don't know?" Inge's head nearly fell to the table. "How can you not know?"

"I only saw her for a minute, okay?" Cara said defensively. "She was dressed in a Santa suit, with a beard and a mustache, fake eyebrows, a hat, white gloves, and a cushion strapped to her stomach—the only real part of her that was actually visible were her eyes."

"Also," Alice said, sounding slightly bored, "what does it matter if she's the same woman or not?"

"Cara needs closure," Inge said simply.

"Okay!" Alice banged her fist on the table. "Enough now! I have been extremely patient with you people. You are my beloved almost-sisters, and I was confident that you were bound to see the light *sometime*, but I guess I was wrong."

27

Cara frowned. "What are you talking about?"

"I have a question," Alice said. "Or rather, a riddle. Picture four women—young, urban, *educated* women. They are having lunch at what is considered to be a reasonably upscale restaurant in the city. They get to talking. They want some information. They spend hours debating their issue, they stare at a picture on a cardboard children's book, endlessly." She lifted her hand in the air. "Now, here's my question. And mind you, we're talking the twenty-first century here, not the nineteenth. What inexhaustible source of information are these friends forgetting to consult?"

"The...uh...Internet?" Cara said.

"Yes, the Internet!" Alice hit the table again. "For God's sake, Google the damn girl already!"

"Good point," Cara admitted.

"And welcome to our digital abode," said Alice, bringing out her phone, "my dear Neanderthals." She took a minute to enter the name. "Here." She looked smug as she handed the phone to Cara.

Inge leaned over to look at the tiny screen. "Wow," she said. "There's like a million hits."

"Told you she was famous," said Myra.

Cara opened the writer's official website.

"Look at her bio page," said Inge. "Maybe there's something there about her personal life."

"She has a partner," Myra said.

"A *partner?*" said Inge. "Is that not the closeted lesbian's word for girlfriend?"

"Ms. Donovan lives," read Cara from the screen, "in the Hollywood Hills with her longtime partner and their two dogs."

"Hollywood Hills?" Alice said. "So what's she doing in our little country by the sea?"

"She lives here now," Myra said. "She traveled to the Netherlands to meet her European fan base and then a year or so later she moved here. Well, half moved here. She spends a few months of the year in California."

"So why Holland? Why Amsterdam? Why not Paris? Or London?"

"Because," Myra said, "she fell in love. That's why."

Cara stared at her. "In love? Who did she fall in love with?"

"With all of us!" Myra stuck her nose up in the air. "She *adores* us. She adores our countryside and our sea. She loves our canals and our windmills. Most of all, she loves our quaint, yellow light when the sun sets. She says it makes her want to take up painting."

Cara grabbed her sister's arm. "Myra," she said, "what the hell? Do you know her? Like personally?"

Myra shrugged. "Sadly, no. I just read up on her. And I YouTubed her to death for a while, to be honest. There's something about her that makes me wonderfully drowsy, as she talks in that cute American accent of hers about kids and being an artist and what it's like to live in two different worlds. She's…what's the word…*soothing*. Jude Donovan puts me to sleep the way her books do my kids."

"So what about the partner?" Cara wanted to hold Myra upside down and shake the information out of her.

"I don't know anything about that," Myra said. "I guess she brought him with her when she moved here. That would seem logical. Then again, maybe she left him behind in the Hollywood Hills. She doesn't talk about personal stuff much."

"So you have all this completely irrelevant information about her, but you don't know if she's gay?" Inge said.

"Why would I? How was *I* supposed to know my baby sister would get the hots for her?"

"I thought the word partner was used mostly by forty-year-old women who are uncomfortable using the term boyfriend," said Alice.

"Nonsense," Inge said. "She's definitely gay." She took the phone from Cara and looked at the photo gallery again. "I totally see it now."

"How can you see something like that?" Alice asked. "I can never tell, not unless they have crew cuts and wear flannel shirts." She paused. "And keys on chains. I nearly fell off my chair when Arend told me about Cara. How could she be…you know? The way she looks?"

"Why?" Cara said. "Because I'm blond?"

"Well…no." Alice shrugged. "You know very well what I mean. It's the way you carry your blondness—it's those damp tendrils of hair around your ears, your subtle makeup, your long-leggedness. It's that whole delicate, feminine, chiffon vibe you send out."

"Chiffon vibe?" Inge turned to Alice. "What the hell—"

"First of all," Cara said, "thank you, I think. Second of all, you guys are a bunch of horrible bigots, and finally, it makes no difference what she is. She could have a thing with Bunny himself for all I care."

"Bunny is a girl," Myra said to nobody in particular.

Inge turned to Cara. "Aren't you curious?"

"I thought I was responsible for getting her fired," Cara said. "For rendering her homeless and starving. Now that I know she's famous and filthy rich, I can stop worrying about that. I'm letting it go. Closure has been had." She handed the phone back to Alice. "Now let's talk about something else."

"Right." Myra got up. "Something else indeed. I need to use the restroom." She looked at Cara. "Come with me, okay?"

"That always weirds me out," Alice said, "women going to the bathroom together." Inge shrugged, picked up her knife, stuck it in a slice of brie, and put it in her mouth.

Once they were in the restroom, looking at their faces in the mirror above the sink, Myra turned to Cara. "Look," she said. "I don't know what the hell is going on with you and Jude Donovan, but if you really want to know who she is, you can find her at De Paddestoel tomorrow—the children's bookstore. You know where it is, right? It has this wildly decorated window full of balloons and garlands and stuffed animals."

Cara nodded. "What's she doing there?"

"Duh! She's promoting her new book."

"Don't tell me." Cara cocked her head. "Is it...*Bunny Solves a Murder*?"

"Actually," Myra said, "it's *Bunny Finds a Friend*."

Cara didn't know what to say to that.

"The store opens at four. I didn't want to tell you in front of them." Myra nudged toward the door. "Inge seems to be coming on a little strong today."

"Will you be there?" Cara pointed to Myra's bulging belly. "Considering you're the chief producer of Ms. Donovan's fan base?"

Myra shook her head. "We can't fit it into our schedule. Saturdays are a bit crazy. In fact, the whole day is one long rush hour."

"I see," said Cara.

"Make no mistakes about this, Cara." Myra wiggled her finger in Cara's face. "This woman is like a God to anybody under the age of six."

She was early, but even so, there was a line waiting, outside the children's bookstore, that meandered all the way down to the Spiegelgracht. There were dozens of kids, screaming, holding Bunny books. They carried bags that no doubt contained drawings and papier-mâché rabbits for the person Myra had referred to as their God.

From the end of the line, the bookstore was nowhere near visible. Cara's heart sank. How long would she have to wait before she was inside? And how would they even be able to fit all these people into the store? It didn't seem that large from the outside—long but narrow. She left the queue and walked in the direction of the bookstore until she was facing it from across the street. She stood for a while, staring at the Bunny-themed window and the cardboard cutouts of Jude Donovan's lovely face. It was pretty impressive. But now what? She wasn't going to spend her day standing in line here. And even if she did, wouldn't it be weird that she was there alone? Shouldn't she have borrowed one of Myra's kids?

Maybe she could wait outside the store until later, she considered, hoping to meet Jude as she came out with a big fat check in her hand. She felt ridiculous when she remembered how worried she had been about Jude starving after being fired from her gig. She hadn't been fired, of course—her performance had probably been a one-time thing. She might have made a tour, visiting random malls throughout the country. A present to her doting audience, to the parents of her fans, who knew, but had to keep secret, that their kid had actually sat on Jude Donovan's lap without even knowing it.

She saw one of her coworkers from the pizza place whizzing by on his bike. He waved, and a thought struck her. She should distinguish herself from the common people somehow. She should gain access to the store by *delivering* something. Something without which Ms. Donovan's performance was going to end in disaster. She thought long and hard—what was it that any reading for children couldn't do without? Children, naturally. A bomb threat? She dismissed this, for obvious reasons. She started pacing up and down the sidewalk, then stopped to think, leaning against a giant, plastic ice cream cone outside a snackbar. She stared at the little bookshop across the wide street, the noise of the traffic washing over her. She realized that she wasn't exactly the world's most inventive person. All she could think of was actually delivering a pizza. But she didn't even know whether the slender Jude ever ate pizza. Maybe she lived on green tea and soybeans. If only she had Alice's phone now, so she could consult the bio page to see if it said anything about her diet.

She considered that she might be going insane. She knew that somewhere in her conscious mind, the question why she was so desperate to meet Jude Donovan was demanding to be answered, but she chose, for now, to ignore this.

Precious time was being wasted. She'd simply have to risk it.

She ran to catch a tram.

Chapter 4

IT WAS ALMOST THREE THIRTY, and the store was still closed. Through the window, Cara saw an old woman with her hair piled up in a bun, busy stacking Bunny books in a helix shape. Cara tapped on the glass door with her fingernail. The woman looked up, but she shook her head. Cara tapped again, a little louder this time.

"We're closed," the woman mouthed. But she walked up to the door anyway. "Were you sent by the agency?" she shouted through the closed door.

Cara didn't know what that meant. She shook her head and put down her bag on the sidewalk. She fished a napkin and a pen out of her pocket, wrote the word delivery on it, and held it against the window. The woman with the bun unlocked the door and opened it about an inch. As if on cue, the waiting children began to howl and push each other forward.

"Hey!" Cara said. "Back off! If you don't stay where you are..." She considered telling them that she had the power to throw Bunny under a bus in the next volume, but she reconsidered. "Quiet!" she shouted instead. "It's almost time! The quieter you are, the sooner this door will open!"

"It's okay," she heard one parent say to another, "she's with the store."

In the meantime, the woman with the bun had closed the door and walked back to her books. Cara tapped on the glass again. The old woman was clearly getting agitated. She shook her head, touched her hair bun, walked back to the door, and opened it once again, only slightly.

"What is it?" she said. "Can't you see we're closed?"

"I have a special delivery," Cara said, pointing to the plastic bag, that she now realized looked far more like an ordinary delivery, and that inconveniently carried the logo of the pizza place.

"Pizza?" the old woman said, pointing to the bag. "We didn't order any."

Cara fished a fake bill out of the bag and looked at it. "This is for a Mr. Donovan."

"A *Ms.* Donovan by any chance?" the old lady asked.

Cara looked at the receipt again. "Sorry, yes," she said innocently. "Ms. Donovan. Is that you?"

The old woman brought her face so close to the door that her considerable nose stuck out of the opening. She sniffed. "Ms. Donovan is our guest at the store today. I'm Mrs. Beldam, the store owner. As you can see there are quite a few young readers looking forward to seeing her. I find it hard to believe that Ms. Donovan would order a pizza no more than half an hour before her performance."

"You know what stars are like," Cara said. She shrugged. "Elvis used to have twenty hamburger menus delivered to his dressing room before he started a show."

The expression on Mrs. Beldam's face turned from annoyed to startled.

"Not that I want to compare Ms. Donovan to Elvis, of course," Cara hastened to add. "She's much...well...thinner.

Also, I'm pretty sure she can't sing." She wiped her forehead with the back of her hand. "Not that I've actually heard her sing—I mean, I don't want to jump to conclusions here. She could have a great voice for all I know, and I've never been a great fan of Elvis myself—there was just something about him that never..." She looked pleadingly at Mrs. Beldam, sensing that something cosmically important would go wrong if she didn't let her in. "It was the suits, I guess." She blew a strand of hair from her forehead. "So white. And then all those fringes and tassels—"

"Hello!" Mrs. Beldam put an end to Cara's bizarre monologue with an angry frown, the joining of her wildly untrimmed eyebrows giving her a strange, owl-like expression. "Miss?" she said. "Why don't you give me the bag, okay? Just hand it to me, and then I will make sure that Ms. Donovan gets it." She stretched out her hand, but Cara swung the bag out of her reach.

"I'm very sorry," she said, "but I really..." She smiled conspiratorially. "The thing is, Ms. Donovan always insists on meeting the person who delivers her pre-performance pizza."

Cara saw Mrs. Beldam's doubts about her sanity grow.

"Young lady, you can either leave the bag with me," she said, "or leave with the bag. It's up to you, and you have about..." she looked at her watch, "...five seconds to make up your mind."

From a door at the far end of the store, a woman walked in the room. Cara could only vaguely make out her features, but she could see that she was addressing Mrs. Beldam, who turned to answer her.

Cara couldn't hear what they were saying, but Mrs. Beldam stuck her finger through the door, pointing to Cara and her bag. This was probably a colleague, who'd been somewhere in the back and had heard them arguing.

The newcomer walked toward the door and stood there for a while, amidst the Bunny book piles and the brightly colored miniature tables and chairs, peering through the window. And the remarkable thing was, from where Cara was standing, she was exactly in line with one of the cardboard cutouts of the face in the window. And there was no mistaking it. The faces were identical. The woman who was staring at her from behind the glass was no shopkeeper—she was, in fact, the wildly popular author herself, Jude Donovan. But although it was obvious that Jude was quite gorgeous, it still wasn't clear to Cara if she was also the Santa who'd been haunting her. She had simply seen too little of her that day to be able to tell. It made her all the more determined to find out.

Cara saw Jude Donovan's lips curl up in a smile. She came closer, until she had reached the door. Mrs. Beldam stepped aside. Jude pushed the door open a little further, ducking when she heard the children begin to holler.

"You'd better come in fast," Jude said. She opened the door wider and Cara, who was beginning to consider that she might be dreaming all this, slipped inside. Mrs. Beldam came rushing forward, locking the door behind her.

Once inside, standing so close to Jude, Cara felt hopelessly shy. She had no idea what to say, having failed to consider what she might do if her plan actually worked.

"This is my assistant," Jude said to Mrs. Beldam. "Is the suit in the back?"

"I'm your...assistant," Cara repeated, dumbfounded.

"The suit, right. Come with me," Mrs. Beldam said to Cara, grabbing her arm.

"The suit?" Cara was too distracted to formally introduce herself. "What is this suit you speak of?"

Jude smiled. "Funny. You'd better get ready, we're running late."

Mrs. Beldam looked at Cara as they were walking to the back of the store and shook her head. "Why didn't you tell me? Why didn't you simply say who you were? We were actually beginning to wonder whether you'd show up at all. I would have let you in straight away if you hadn't gone on about your silly delivery. What was that about anyway?"

"The...uh..." Cara said, "...silly delivery, yes." She inhaled deeply. "I'm sorry about that. It was a joke. But not a very funny one, I see that now."

Mrs. Beldam opened a door to a tiny hallway that led to a small kitchen on the one, and a narrow, spiral staircase on the other side. She began to walk up the stairs, looking behind her almost constantly to make sure that Cara was still following her. Climbing was a considerable effort for Mrs. Beldam—she was moving slowly, panting a little and leaning heavily on the banister. Once upstairs, Cara took a couple of steps forward, the wooden floorboards creaking beneath her feet. She tried to survey the room, but it was too dark to see much. Mrs. Beldam flipped a switch on the wall and a faint, orange glow from the light bulb that was dangling from the ceiling settled on the cramped space. There was a musty smell, something that Cara couldn't quite make out—something stale and yet sweet.

"There isn't that much space to move around," Mrs. Beldam said. "This is mainly a storage room."

It was hardly more than a broom closet, Cara thought, with an *actual* broom, lying on the floor. The room was packed. It was packed with furniture, boxes full of books, more boxes on shelves with unknown contents, toys, balloons, stuffed animals, a year's supply of coffee and tea. A clothes rack full of kid's clothing, mostly coats and sweatshirts, was wedged between the slanting ceiling and the wall. Cara assumed that these were garments accidentally left in the store by their owners, but there was no way of knowing for sure. Maybe Mrs. Beldam was one of those old ladies who ate small children. Cara stared at her, at the wrinkled face, the dark clothing, the considerable nose. She almost jumped when Mrs. Beldam picked up the broom from the floor and walked toward her. She swallowed. Was she…flying off? To Cara's relief, the old woman didn't actually *mount* the broom.

"Better get this out of the way," Mrs. Beldam said, "before someone trips over it."

Cara was sure of one thing only. She wanted to get out of here. She felt that there was some voodoo ritual in the air that she wanted no part of.

"Look…" she said. "Here's the thing…"

Mrs. Beldam took something, covered in a plastic wrap, from the top shelf and pushed it into Cara's arms. Inside the wrapper lay something fluffy, and for a second, Cara was afraid it was someone's dead pet. She wondered what she was getting herself into. Sure, the famous writer was downstairs. The only thing separating them was a small staircase and a plywood door. But when it came down to it, what did Cara really know about Jude Donovan or any bizarre issues she might have? Things that hadn't been on her website because there was no page for icky fetishes.

"We had it cleaned like Ms. Donovan asked," Mrs. Beldam said. "I don't think it's been worn for quite some time. But it's still in good condition. I'll leave you to it then. Please, hurry."

She walked down the stairs, leaving Cara alone. Cara didn't really know what to do but to unwrap the package. She tore off the wrap and something fluffy and white fell to the floor. And then she finally understood what was going on and slapped herself on the forehead. Even as it lay there, she realized what it was. What it *had* to be. How stupid of her not to get it right away. It was a Bunny suit! She was supposed to put it on and entertain the children! Both Jude and the old lady had mistaken her for the hired rabbit. She burst out laughing, the sound ricocheting off the walls.

"Is everything all right up there?" Mrs. Beldam shouted from the bottom of the stairs.

"Fine," Cara shouted back. "I'll be down in just a second." She shrugged. "Ah, what the hell," she said to herself. She might as well step up to the plate now that she'd come this far. There was every chance that the real Bunny impersonator would show up, but they would have to deal with that when the time came. She was inside the store, she had access to the beautiful Jude, and who knows what else might happen on this bizarre, adventurous day. So she'd have to entertain a thousand toddlers, so what? She broke out in a sweat and tried to think of something else.

She took off her coat and shoes, opened the zipper on the suit, stepped into the fuzzy white feet, and wrapped the suit around her. She didn't know whether it was a one-size-fits-all kind of thing, but once she had it on, she realized it was exactly right for her. She was reminded of the day at the mall, and she wondered whether it was somehow Jude's and her fate to see each other only in costumes that revealed nothing but their eyes and mouths.

The floppy ears were enormous. So were the feet. She considered taking her glasses off, remembering that rabbits were known for their good eyesight on account of all the carrots they eat. But since there was already every chance she'd fall down the stairs because of the feet, she decided to leave them on, at least for now.

As luck had it, she managed to get down in one piece. She felt ridiculous, but both Mrs. Beldam and Jude were very pleased with what they saw when she presented herself to them. Mrs. Beldam, glad to have at least this worry out of the way, excused herself, remembering that she needed to go up to the attic again to get more copies of Jude's bestsellers, *Bunny Has a Boo-Boo* leading the pack. She was obviously counting on making a killing today.

"Look at you, you're just perfect," Jude said, once they were alone, "as Bunnies go." She smiled, looking Cara up and down. "Personally," she added, "I thought you were more perfect before you had the suit on."

Was Jude blushing? Cara was feeling even more self-conscious in her lagomorph getup than before. How could she respond to such obvious flirting now that she was a freaking rabbit?"

She looked at Jude and nodded. "Thank you," she said. "Perhaps I should introduce myself."

"No need." Jude smiled. "Bunny, right?"

"Uh...right."

"The agency sent you, right?"

"The...uh...agency," Cara said.

"You *are* with the agency?"

"I'm actually more of an...independent Bunny," Cara said.

She glanced at Jude, who was wearing jeans, boots, and a low-cut black top, that would have been a little too sexy if it hadn't been set off by a dressy grey jacket. Resting between her collarbones was a large, silver necklace—an intricate design of birds in flight that reminded Cara of the yin and yang symbol. Jude was slightly shorter than Cara, and curvier than her slender form had initially revealed. Her hair was just brushing the tip of her shoulders. It was very straight and almost black. Her hazel eyes rested on Cara with that intense gaze that Cara now realized had also struck her during their brief encounter at the store. Her hands were quite elegant, with long fingers and perfectly groomed nails. There were no rings. She had straight, very white teeth. There was a slight scar on her left temple that only seemed to emphasize the flawlessness of her skin.

It wasn't that it hit Cara like a ton of bricks, it was more of a slow burning realization - Jude Donovan was *definitely* the Santa from the store.

"An independent Bunny?"

"Why all the questions?" Cara asked. "You ordered a Bunny, and here I am." She curtsied again. For old times' sake.

"The funny thing is," said Jude with a mocking expression, "that I just got a call from the agency telling me that my ordered Bunny is home in bed with the flu, and that sadly they couldn't find anybody to replace her at such short notice."

"The flu, huh?" Cara realized they were getting nowhere. "Bummer."

"So…" Jude shrugged, "you showing up here is quite the mystery."

Cara realized it was time for a change of tactics. "Can I be perfectly honest here?"

Jude nodded. "Sounds like a plan."

"Do you know who I am?"

"Well," said Jude, "it wouldn't have taken me as long to figure it out as it *has*, if you'd been wearing your shiny badge like any good civil servant must." She smiled. "But it dawned on me eventually. I recognized your…" she cleared her throat "…features." She looked at Cara as if she wanted to eat her, one delicious bite at a time. Cara, feeling ridiculous and extremely hot in her costume, writhed uncomfortably. Were there bugs in the suit? But then she remembered that Mrs. Beldam had had it dry cleaned. The itch was her own.

"Right," she said. "The features."

Jude grinned. "Don't tell me you were ordered by the court to deliver me a pizza?"

Cara watched the kids outside pressing their faces against the window. It was close to four now, and they demanded to get what was rightfully theirs. God knows they had waited long enough. Some parents may have actually slept in front of the store that night to make sure their precious offspring would get to meet the great rabbit.

"Don't they frighten you a little?" Cara said. "In these numbers?"

"They're fans," Jude said. "I adore them."

"I'm not very good with kids myself," Cara confessed.

"Sure you are," Jude said. "You have to be. My reputation seems to be in your hands once again, and I *urge* you not to screw up another one of my gigs. Take some responsibility here. You made your bed, now lie in it."

"Don't worry," Cara said, bowing her head so that her ears flopped forward. "I will do you proud."

Jude took one of the ears in her hands and let the fur glide through her fingers. Cara couldn't decide whether the fact that she found this to be highly arousing made her into some sort of pervert. A lot of things were happening today that were confusingly unprecedented.

"You know what the secret is?" Jude said, letting go of the ear. "Take them seriously. Respect them, and they will respond in turn."

"Aren't you going to ask me why I came here in the first place?" Cara said.

"We have little time," Jude warned her. "The window will only hold them for so long."

"Okay then," Cara said. "I'll get to the point. I wanted to apologize. I've been trying to find you to tell you that. I was rude. I was going through some stuff that day, but it was wrong of me to take it out on you."

That's okay," Jude said. "I seem to remember I wasn't exactly a lady myself."

Cara shook her head. "You offered to have the stick removed from my ass."

Jude smiled. "Shame on me."

"I didn't know who you were," Cara said. "That you were this great celebrity, I mean. A great, *American* celebrity. My sister told me. Her kids are devoted fans. So I came up with a ruse to see you. A cunning and devious plan."

The children's voices were sounding louder now that they were catching a glimpse of Bunny. It was beginning to get difficult for the parents to keep them in line.

"This was your cunning and devious plan?" Jude asked, ignoring the outside noise. "Misleading Mrs. Beldam into thinking I ordered a pizza?" She shook her head. "I'm beginning to wonder if you're even worthy of your badge."

"I didn't say I was good at it," Cara said. "Also, there's no more badge."

"I see. What happened, did you get a promotion?"

Cara shook her head. "It's a long story," she said. It was actually a very short story, but she wasn't about to discuss the deplorable state of her career with the most successful person she'd ever met.

"So what about the documents I delivered that day?"

Jude shrugged. "What about them?"

Cara didn't know how to ask what the reason was for her to be summoned by the court without seeming rude and intrusive. And then, did she even want to know? What if it was something that would make the wonderful tingling feeling she was having underneath all that horrible fur disappear?

"You're wondering why I got them," Jude said." She smiled. "What my crime is, as it were."

Cara nodded. "Actually, yes. But you don't have to tell me, of course. Not unless you want to."

"It's okay," Jude said. "It's not a secret. We all get to that point sometimes where murder seems to be the only solution to a problem. I'm sure you've been there yourself. I simply acted on instinct. What I hadn't realized was that it would feel so incredibly good. That it would come so naturally to me. That after that first time, there's really no going back."

Cara stared at her in horror and stepped away from her, nearly knocking over a pile of books.

"You're very easy to fool, aren't you?" Jude burst out laughing.

Cara wanted to punch her, but she produced an embarrassed smile instead.

Jude's face turned grave. "If you must know, there's a bit of a problem concerning a plagiarism suit. Someone is trying to convince the court that I stole my Bunny stories from him. I'll spare you the details. It's not very interesting."

"I see," Cara said.

"For the record, it's all nonsense. This whole affair has been a bit of a nightmare, but I'm sure it will all be over soon."

Mrs. Beldam came back with the books. "It's almost time," she declared solemnly.

"It's almost time," Jude repeated. Her words seemed both ominous and soothing, as if their meaning extended far beyond the simple fact that she was ready to meet her fans. "Remember, we're in this together now."

"I'm up to the task," Cara said. "Although I'm not exactly familiar with any Bunny lingo or special features."

"There are two things you have to remember," said Jude. "Bunny is prone to socializing with other species, much to the dismay of her bourgeois and irritatingly overprotective parents. And she's always looking for ways to eat carrot cake."

"Carrot cake," Cara said. "Got it."

"Fans tend to *bring* carrot cake to readings. Often made by five-year-olds. Soggy. With sprinkles." Jude smiled. "*Bon appetit.*"

"Yuk," said Cara. "I don't even like carrot cake made by pastry chefs, let alone—"

"Tough luck!" said Jude. "You know what? Come through for me today, and I'll pay you the going rate *and* I'll take you out for coffee when we're done, okay?"

Cara smiled. "Deal." Then she frowned. "There's a going rate?"

"Or maybe drinks, if you prefer that. Your choice."

"Drinks. I would definitely prefer drinks."

It seemed to Cara that having drinks would take longer and had a different weight to it. Going for coffee was innocent; going for drinks could be the stepping stone to pretty much anything. She was beginning to get very excited about the way things were developing, but there was just one more thing she needed to get out of the way. If it was inappropriate, so be it.

"Will that be okay, though," she said, eyeing Jude innocently, "with your longtime partner?"

Jude stared at her for a second. "With my…what?"

Cara shrugged. "It's just that I read on your website that you live in the Hollywood Hills with your partner and two dogs."

"Wow." Jude chortled, which made Cara feel like a three-year-old. "You learned the whole page by heart?"

"No," Cara said, "just that particular bit."

"So?"

"Nothing." Cara shrugged. "I know you live in the Netherlands part of the year. And I was just wondering if your…you know…man, or husband, will be picking you up and joining us for…well…whatever it is we'll be having." Her heart was pounding in her chest. "That would be fun, I suppose. To meet him."

She blushed. She hated herself.

"Right," said Jude. "The thing is, the information on the website regarding my situation is a little outdated." She cleared her throat. "Things…" Her voice trailed off.

"What?"

She flinched. "This isn't something I want to get into right now, okay? Let's go with the simple version and say that things changed."

"Okay, sure." Cara nodded. "Things changed. They always do, don't they? Usually when you least want them to."

"I left California when my marriage ended," Jude said simply. "It's no secret. It's just not public knowledge."

And yet, Cara thought, my sister knew all about it.

"Laurie and I split up and I needed a change of pace," Jude continued. "New horizons, that sort of thing." She smiled. "Turned out that your horizon was the prettiest of them all. It's the light, you see. At dusk. It's captivating."

Cara couldn't focus on this most romantic of revelations the way she might have done, being a fan of the dusk herself. Her focus was on something else. A name that made her head spin. *Laurie*! Not John, not Brad, not Michael. Laurie! And not just any Laurie—a Laurie she had *left*.

And that was all they had time for.

"Ladies," Mrs. Beldam shouted. "In three, two, one!"

She opened the door and there they were, dozens of screaming, stampeding children who almost knocked her flat.

Cara wasn't prepared for what happened next. She thought they'd all be storming toward Jude, but as it turned out, it wasn't Jude they were after at all. They were far more interested in Bunny, their adorable furry idol, than in the author who had brought that furry idol to life. They threw themselves at Cara. She tried to remember feverishly what exactly it was that bunnies *do*. She needed some kind of act here, something to give them their money's worth. The only bunny she'd ever known was Konijn, the pet rabbit she'd had as a child—and all he did was twitch his nose and hop. Hop! She crouched down and gave it a go, not just the hopping, but even the twitching of the nose. The kids went crazy. They shoved carrots in her face, which she took between her teeth and started munching on. The bravest ones among them climbed on her back. They stroked her fur. They played with her ears. They gave her presents and drawings. She thanked them and admired their art in a falsetto voice—hoping she would sound like what these kids might imagine Bunny to sound like.

They loved her. They had a blast. And so did she.

Every time she managed to come up for air, she'd steal a glance at Jude, who was watching her from a distance. She liked what she read on Jude's face. It made her try even harder to do her proud.

By the time Cara finally calmed the little fans down and it was time for Jude to start reading, they were exhausted. They sat on the floor in a half circle, close to Jude's chair, and all the while, they listened speechlessly, many with their mouths open—you could hear a pin drop. Mrs. Beldam went wild with her little camera.

Hours later, when peace had finally returned to the little bookstore and Cara was once again dressed like a human being, Mrs. Beldam practically pushed Cara and Jude out the door.

"But...this!" Cara protested, pointing to the battlefield the young visitors had left behind.

"This will be just fine," Mrs. Beldam assured her. "Someone's coming over later to help me, okay?" She nudged them toward the exit. "Now you two kids run along. I'm sure you have better things to do with your time than to hang around here." She looked at them almost lovingly.

Am I crazy, Cara thought, slightly amused, or does Mrs. Beldam know exactly what's going on here?

The streets were quieter now, the sun had set, leaving a faint pink glow on the horizon. They were walking side by side, until Jude stopped and extended her hand. "I'm Jude, by the way."

Cara placed her hand in Jude's, purposefully holding it a little too long. "I'm Cara."

"Yes," Jude said, "Cara. Of course. I've come up with a hundred names in my head, and not one seemed to be right for you. Cara is perfect."

Cara became a little light headed. Jude had thought about her long enough to come up with a hundred names for her?

"The name is very rare in the Netherlands," she said. "My grandmothers were called Carolina and Rachel—my parents decided to get a little creative."

"Then I guess I was wrong," Jude said. "It thought it was Irish. It makes me think of clover and green pastures."

Cara shrugged. "There's no reason why it can't now."

The night was cool and crisp. Cara felt, or maybe more imagined, that there was a touch of spring in the air, even though it was only February. The darkness had felt different these past nights, thinner almost, as if it were already beginning to surrender to a force it was bound to succumb to.

"I like walking through the city at night," Jude said. "I need to unwind after a day like this. I enjoy it, but it's exhausting."

Cara nodded. She was quite happy to have Jude to herself, to walk by her side. She stole a glance at her from time to time, hoping to be inconspicuous. Maybe it was the fact that she was dealing with a celebrity that made her cautious where she was used to being bold. It still wasn't 100 percent clear to her what was going on here. Jude had flirted with and wanted to work with her, and she admitted to having thought about her. But that wasn't enough for Cara to make out whether this was some sort of date or a simple stroll with a friendly stranger.

She put her hands in the pockets of her coat. "Me too," she said. "I like it too."

They walked in the direction of the Herengracht. Jude's pace was brisk. She struck Cara as that cliché of the active, outdoorsy person she had always admired but had never been able to become. She'd had this image of Jude's life, the life of a famous writer residing in the Hollywood Hills with a partner, dogs, horses maybe. Cara's mind had constructed a detailed picture—the Tudor-style house, the massive study where Jude worked, the walls lined with bookcases, elaborate chandeliers decorating the high ceiling. She had imagined Jude and her partner going on long hikes, entertaining guests, spending their evenings on the impressive porch, watching the sun disappear behind the mountains. The picture was probably inaccurate. She had never actually been to California, and what she knew about Californian homes was what she'd seen on television. It didn't matter now, anyway, since Jude was obviously more impressed by the narrow streets and canals of Amsterdam than she was by the impressive mountains in her own land.

And yet, it didn't feel as though it had made her any less unattainable. She'd felt so close to her at the bookstore, but now, Cara was afraid she'd fallen into that old trap of reading too much into things that were really quite innocent. It was a thing with her. She tended to fall too hard, too soon. It was how she set herself up for disappointments. Even now that she was here, walking right by her side, Jude seemed as elusive as ever.

Or was she?

They turned to each other at the exact same moment. Their eyes locked, then Jude looked away. Cara took a deep breath.

"What's wrong?" Jude asked, slowing down.

"Nothing," Cara said. She felt like a sixteen-year-old at a school dance, hiding a crush on a hot girl, wondering if life would ever become simple.

"Tell me, okay?"

"You don't want to know."

Jude stopped abruptly. Cara nearly collided with her.

"Trust me," Jude said. "I do."

Cara started walking again—she wanted to take Jude to the crossing of the Reguliersgracht and the Herengracht to show her the spot where you could see fifteen bridges over the canals in one fell swoop. At this time of night, the bridges were illuminated, making it one of the most romantic spots in the city.

The moon had come out from behind the clouds, bathing everything in a pale, bluish light. Cara shivered. There was a promise to the night that made her soar. She was no stranger to this feeling, and she had always made the most of it, but tonight, she had no idea what to do about it.

"I'm not the most steady person in the world," she said, as Jude caught up with her.

"So?"

"I've fucked up every relationship I ever had."

Jude seemed to give this some thought. "Maybe," she said finally, "you've just never been with the right person."

"Can I be honest?"

Jude nodded. "Sure."

Cara stopped in her tracks in the middle of the bridge from where she was dying to show Jude the view. "First, I want to show you something," she said. They turned to the water and Cara pointed to the six arched bridges in a row, and then to the other six, and then to the left, where there were two more. "The bridge we're standing on is the fifteenth," she said. "Have you ever seen this before?"

Jude shook her head. "I can't believe this city," she said. "I felt as though I was walking through some kind of fairytale the first time I came here. The atmosphere is so overwhelming, so different from anything I have ever known. I fell in love as soon as I had taken my first stroll."

As they both turned around, leaning against the iron railing of the bridge, the carillon of Westerkerk began to chime, as if to emphasize the city's allure.

"You were going to be honest," Jude reminded Cara. She looked at her expectantly.

Cara realized that Jude was cold. Her face was paler now, and she was shivering as she put her hands in the pockets of her coat. Cara wished she was brave enough to take them into her own pockets and keep them warm there. But she was shy. There were all these people here—day and night, there were people here—there was traffic, there was noise, there were the bells of streetcars and churches ringing, and the carillon chiming, and the canalboats whispering. There were what seemed like a million people on bicycles passing by.

"I've been trying to find you for a reason," she said.

"To apologize, right?" Jude's mocking smile was back.

"You really enjoy torturing me, don't you?"

"You make it so easy," Jude said. "But I'll have mercy on you, okay? Let me help you out here. You were trying to find me, because you felt the same thing I did that day at the store. That while we were arguing, there was something there, beneath the surface, something that was warm and tingly and that might be worth exploring."

Cara nodded.

"So what can we do about that?"

Cara shrugged.

"Cara," Jude said. "Come on. I'm sure we can think of *something*."

Jude made a half turn. Now they were face to face. She pushed her body gently against Cara's, leaving no doubt as to her intentions.

"We're standing on an illuminated bridge," Cara said. She giggled, both nervous and amused.

"So?" Jude said. "This is Amsterdam, remember? Anything goes. Light is good."

Cara put her hands on Jude's hips, but she couldn't actually feel anything through the fabric of Jude's quilted coat. Jude, being bolder, stroked Cara's hair, her hand lingering on her neck, on her jaw. Then she moved her hand toward Cara's mouth and slowly ran a thumb across her lips. Cara forgot to breathe. Jude moved her hand away, then she took both Cara's hands in hers and held them. She looked at them, brought them to her face, kissed the wrists, kissed the fingers, and intertwined them with her own. Jude seemed to want to touch every piece of exposed skin she could find. Cara had never felt so desirable. She looked into Jude's eyes. They were darker now. She knew what that meant, and she thought it best not to move, not to speak.

Jude pushed herself against Cara with more force, and then boldly started kissing her. Cara, taken by surprise at the depth of this first kiss, felt her knees start to give out. There was no careful planning, no getting to know a new, strange mouth—Jude's kiss was a complete surrender; slow, sensual and deep. Cara felt as though she'd been standing in the cold for a lifetime and was now sinking down on a soft bed, covered by the warmest, fluffiest quilt she had ever felt. She reached out her arms, but Jude took her wrists and pinned her hands on the railing of the bridge, resting them on the cold metal. At the same time, she ground her hips against Cara's. All the while, she never broke the kiss. Cara was rendered motionless, and she relished in the feeling of having no choice but to meet Jude's hungry mouth and to make love to it.

All thoughts were pushed to the background as her body took over and silenced her mind. When they finally came up for air, Cara blinked, wondering if what she saw was true—that the world had taken on a new, brighter color. People were walking and cycling over the bridge, but nobody paid any attention to them. Perhaps, seeing two women make out in one of the busiest spots in the city was something they were quite accustomed to, and completely comfortable with.

"Jesus," Cara said. "Ever hear of spontaneous human combustion?"

She looked out over the water, trying to catch her breath. A canalboat appeared from under the bridge. A man waved at her from inside. He seemed to have a camera in his hand. She briefly wondered what her sisters would think if they saw her on YouTube tonight, making out with Jude in public. She turned around, leaning against the bridge for support. An elderly woman in a bright-yellow coat scurried past them, eying them suspiciously. Jude tipped an imaginary hat to her. Then she turned back to Cara and smiled.

"I take it you going up in flames would be a good sign?"

Cara nodded. "I've never done this in public with a famous writer before."

Jude took a bow. "I'm proud to be your first one."

Cara wrapped her arms around Jude's neck, pulled her close, and initiated the next kiss. If anything, this one was even better, their embrace making it more intimate. Cara was used to showing a little restraint when she kissed a woman for the first time, getting to know her style. With Jude, the word restraint seemed to have disappeared from the dictionary. Not only did Cara not want to show any, she found herself unable to—it was impossible to not surrender to this most sensual of feelings. Kissing Jude was much more than kissing Jude, Cara realized. It was also more than a prelude to sex. It *was* sex, some kind of miniature version of it. It was feeling what their mouths were doing resonate in her entire body—tingling, pounding, throbbing. And it was no different for Jude, for as Cara felt her arousal build within her, she knew, through her sounds, through the way she moved, that Jude's was building in sync with her own.

But when she felt Jude's knee gently trying to part her legs, her head suddenly became clear. She realized that if she didn't put a stop to this right now, things would get horribly out of hand. She pulled back. Abruptly. Jude kept leaning into her, her head on Cara's shoulder. Cara, hearing Jude's ragged breathing so very close to her ear, fought to keep her self-control, the urge to kiss Jude again almost impossible to resist.

"What's wrong?" Jude said, panting.

"I want to do this more than anything," Cara whispered in her ear. "But not here."

"I'm sorry," Jude said. The spell was broken. She lifted her head off Cara's shoulder and stepped back. She brushed off her coat and ran a hand through her hair. "Me neither," she said, shaking her head. "Making out in public is cheap and tacky." She apologized again. "I got carried away." She reached out her hand and tenderly ran a finger across Cara's cheek. "You're just so very—" She made a sound that was halfway between a moan and a growl.

Cara tried to imitate the sound, and then they laughed together. Cara thought she had never seen anyone look at her quite so lovingly before.

"We need to get out of the cold," she said. "My apartment isn't far."

Jude shook her head. "Let's just walk, okay?" She was blowing on her hands—the temperature was dropping.

Cara followed her down the bridge, less than tempted to spend more time outside. "Why?" she said. "My apartment is near. It's also warm." But she followed Jude anyway.

"My own apartment is actually near here, too," Jude said. "The location is not the point. And while your offer is more than tempting, I think I'll decline."

Cara's heart sank. She declined? After what just happened? Was she a horrible kisser? Was there someone else? Was it a mistake? And if it was, would she *ever* recover?

"You don't want to." She sounded exactly the way she felt—devastated.

"On the contrary," Jude said. "There's nothing I want more right now than for you to take me home and continue what we started." Her eyes were gentle as she looked at Cara. "But as someone who fucked up every relationship she ever had, maybe you should begin this in style."

Cara grinned. "Hasn't that ship sort of sailed?"

"I mean," Jude said, punching her affectionately, "from now on."

Cara nodded. "Maybe. So what are you suggesting?"

"Let's do this right," Jude said. "Let's go on an official date."

Cara stared at the reflection of the trees in the water of the canal and took a second to consider this. "Date?"

"You know. Dressing up? Dinner? Maybe a movie?" Jude put her arm round Cara's shoulder, pulled her close and brought her lips to Cara's ear. "I'm sensing there's more to be had here than getting to second base on a bridge in the freezing cold," she whispered. She looked up at a streetlamp that cast a warm, golden light on them. "No matter how romantic the ambiance."

"Why Ms. Donovan," Cara said, "are you trying to say you want to woo me?"

Jude pulled her arm back. "I can't stand you when you're cocky," she said.

Cara was laughing out loud now. She rested her hand on Jude's shoulder and looked at her. "I want to woo you too," she said, suddenly serious.

They stopped and began to lean into each other again, but just before their lips met, Jude pulled back. "Whoa!" she said. "I don't think this is going to work unless we put a little distance between us." She looked at Cara and shook her head. "I can't be trusted around you. I used to be so respectable, *now* look at me."

Cara sighed. "What about the state you got me in?"

"You do look a little flushed." Jude grinned. "I'm sure it's nothing a cold shower won't cure though."

Cara pushed her teasingly. "You're killing me here."

Jude shook her head. "I hate to think what it would do to Santa's reputation, as well as to my own, if I got myself arrested for indecent exposure." She rested her dark eyes on Cara. "So how about that date?"

Cara nodded. "I would love to go out with you."

Jude took her hand and kissed it. "I promise I will be a perfect lady this time."

"Ugh," Cara said. "Where's the fun in that? Please, promise me you'll be anything but."

Jude laughed. "Don't tempt me, okay? So how about Saturday? Meet me at eight. Here, on the bridge." She cocked her head. "All star-crossed lovers meet on bridges, after all."

Cara nodded. "Eight it is," she said. She leaned over, kissed Jude gently on the cheek, then turned around and walked away.

"Try to behave yourself until then, okay?" Jude called after her.

Cara raised her hand. As she walked to the metro station, she knew, that if she wanted to, she would be able to fly.

Chapter 5

"AND?"

"And what?"

Inge rolled her eyes. "Duh! Did you meet? Was it her? Was Hot Santa, Hot Writer?"

Cara nodded solemnly. "I did, and she was."

"And?"

"And what?"

"Is it like: met her, done her?"

"Don't be vulgar, okay?" Myra shoved Inge. "You're talking about the person my kids adore."

"More importantly," said Cara, "we're talking about my reputation. Which is, as you all know, that of a virtual nun."

Alice frowned. "A virtual nun? Is that a person who'll give you digital absolution?"

"Come on!" Inge rolled her eyes. "Stop kidding around. Cara, tell us—did you at least get to first base?"

"Ah yes." Alice stared off into space. "First base. Good times."

Cara sighed, content rather than irritated. "Before we get ahead of ourselves here, let me tell you that I had the privilege of both watching Ms. Donovan get trampled by a million screaming children, and of walking with her." She didn't feel comfortable revealing that she'd been dressed in a rabbit suit most of the afternoon, afraid it would turn her success story into something that might easily be ridiculed.

They paused as the waitress put down their plates. They were in a new place today, suggested by Inge. It was a low-key venue, with slow service—the staff very young and less than forthcoming. The sisters were sitting in a booth, on faux leather, which Alice complained stuck to her legs so badly that every time she moved, she ripped off a piece of skin. The menu was equally unpretentious, which is why both Cara and Alice made do with coffee and a piece of the *appeltaart*, with a large dollop of whipped cream on top.

"Walking with her?" Inge's face expressed pure disgust.

"Indeed," Cara said. "It was delightful."

"Walking with her?" Inge repeated. "Delightful? What are you, Charlotte fucking Brontë?"

"Far from it." Cara thought back to the very un-Victorian kiss she and Jude had shared. "Although I have to confess to knowing very little about Miss Brontë's love life. To the point where I have no idea if she even had one."

"I thought you were supposed to read that old stuff all the time?" Alice said.

Cara shrugged. "I never really got how any couple made it past all those complicated social codes. All I know is that there was a lot of courting and pining going on, but I'm not sure anybody ever really got down to business. And even if they did, it must have taken them hours to get all those skirts off." She scooped up a spoonful of whipped cream and put it in her mouth, moaning a little as she felt the velvety substance touch her palate. She seemed to be unusually sensitive to anything physically appealing these days, even sugary treats, which she'd never been particularly passionate about before. It was as if Jude's kiss had enhanced all her senses. She wondered longingly what effect sharing more than just a kiss would have on her. The prospect alone made her tingle and rendered her oddly breathless, as if the oxygen were suddenly sucked out of the room.

"You've really thought this through, haven't you?" Inge asked, obviously intrigued. "You do realize that only half the couple would have been wearing skirts?"

"Yeah, right," Cara said. "It was *our* generation that invented the possible coupling of two skirted people." She smiled. "Nobody had ever tried it before. It was quite the eureka moment."

"And besides," said Alice, "men had complicated wardrobes too. Vests, suspenders, waistcoats, neckties, breaches—it can't have been easy getting into *those* pants either."

Myra cleared her throat. "Not that this isn't fascinating," she said, "but let me just steer us back on topic here. Did Ms. Donovan happen to mention when her new book is coming out?"

"No," Cara said. "She did not."

"So what did you talk about?" Alice studied her nails. "Rabbits?"

Cara shrugged. "Life. Literature. The future of the planet."

"Did she like...bring that out in you?" Alice kept probing.

"Why? I talk about life and literature and the future of the planet all the time."

"You do? When?"

"Alice is right," said Myra. "You sound different. More like the eloquent Cara you used to be. I always pegged you for a poet, but lately..." She hummed. "Not so much."

Cara cocked her head. "Thanks."

"I'm just saying that Jude is having a profound effect on you. Already."

You have no idea, Cara thought.

"And that's wonderful," Myra continued. "It's all coming together for you now." She wobbled her head from side to side, trying to see past her stomach. "Could somebody please check if I'm wearing matching shoes? I can't see them, but they feel individually different."

"I'm not going down there," said Inge. "Chances are that if you can't see your feet, you definitely can't wash them."

Alice bent down and looked under the table. "They're identical," she said, pulling a face. "The shoes, I mean. And that's pretty much the only positive thing I can say about them."

"My ankles are a little swollen," Myra explained, "which is why I switched to a more comfortable type of footwear."

"I hope it's all worth it," Alice said.

Inge stiffened. "How can you even say that?" she whispered. "It's worth any sacrifice."

"I'm sorry." Alice shook her head. "I wasn't thinking."

Cara reached out her hand and gently put it on Inge's shoulder. Inge shrugged it off. Something that was dark and grave began to fill the atmosphere, like a toxin.

"I'm almost sorry they're the same," Myra said finally, trying to lighten the mood. "I could have started a new trend." She eyed Cara. "But anyway."

"What?" Cara said.

"I find the idea of you hooking up with Jude Donovan a little out there, frankly. It's like something out of a movie. Surreal."

"It didn't feel surreal at all," Cara said. "It felt very natural. It was as if I'd known her all my life." She smirked, bracing herself for the comments that were bound to follow her uncharacteristic sappiness.

Inge leaned over to the floor, making loud gagging noises.

"You're just jealous." Cara pushed her. "I bet Bart doesn't seem like much of a catch now!"

"Will you be seeing her again?" Myra's eyes grew wide. "Could you...you know, set up a private thing for the kids?"

"I don't know," Cara said. "We're going out for pasta Saturday."

"Don't screw this up, Cara, okay?" Myra shook her head. "Not this time."

෧ ᴗ ꤼ

They had dinner at Magna Plaza, a luxurious shopping mall between the Royal Palace and the New Church. The interior of the nineteenth century, neo-gothic building consisted of a central hall with galleries and two upper floors, surrounded by arcades and crowned by a sunroof. It had a stylish brasserie on the ground floor, with beautiful wooden features, shiny mirrors, and splendid, crystal chandeliers. Cara thought it was a great place for an official first date.

She was happy. It was noisy, it was warm, she had wine, she had spaghetti; and sitting across from her, her eyes sparkling, her long legs occasionally touching her own ankles under the table, was this stunningly gorgeous woman that she was only just getting to know.

Cara looked across the table, hoping to lock eyes with Jude. She was looking breathtaking tonight, without having compromised the corporate look that seemed to be

64

her preferred style. She was casual chic, in a writerly sort of way—a white silk blouse, black cigarette pants, and a similar grey jacket to the one she'd worn at the bookstore. The blouse had one button too many open for this to be an innocent dinner with a new friend, revealing a light swell of the perfect skin, and the tiniest strip of a red lace bra. Cara tried not to stare. Jude's unusual necklace obviously had an adjustable chain, for the pendant now rested not between her collarbones, like last time, but between her breasts. She wore dime-sized, silver hoops in her ears—two in each—and Cara's eyes lingered on them, straying down the curve of Jude's jawline to her delicate neck. Her perfume, something light and floral, wafted toward Cara like a caress. She didn't wear any makeup—the smooth, olive skin obviously not needing any. On her lips, there was a hint of color. Just that.

Cara cleared her throat. She remembered, once again, kissing Jude on the bridge, in the cold night air. She realized that if there were a respectable way to do so, she'd suggest skipping desert and going outside to find out if the magic of that first night was still there. She was as mesmerized by the gorgeous writer now as she was each time they met—she'd actually been counting the hours until their date.

She took a piece of garlic bread from the basket and offered it to Jude, who accepted it with a smile. Cara was reminded that not only was this her favorite restaurant, it was her favorite part of the night, and definitely her favorite part of a relationship. It was all so new and exciting. There were all these things to learn about the woman sitting across from her, and to imagine about her. The fact that she'd kissed Jude once before only heightened her expectations. She loved the blueprint for this kind of night—the playful but polite conversation, the subtle shift to a more personal choice of subject, and then, finally, the stage where the inhibitions dissipated as cheeks became flushed, wine bottles empty, and stares meaningful. Tonight the air was thick and sticky with promise.

Jude looked around. "I've never been here before," she said.

Adults didn't seem to know Jude when there were no kids or Bunny books around. People definitely looked at her, but without recognizing her. She was out of context here, to Cara's relief.

"Isn't it beautiful?" Cara said. "This was once Amsterdam's main post office. It was converted into a shopping mall in the early nineties. The exterior was completely rebuilt, keeping the original decorative elements intact."

"It's wonderful, and very cozy," Jude said. "Grand but intimate, just the way I like it. Do you come here often?"

Cara didn't want to kill the mood by admitting that she tended to take new lovers here, so she shook her head. "Not exactly often. When I go out, it's usually with my sisters, and we tend to select grand café's with fewer tourists—you know, the darker and smaller places, with those frighteningly narrow steps leading down to the restrooms."

Jude took a sip of wine. "Sounds like you guys are pretty tight."

Cara nodded. "It's not always easy, but yes, we're tight."

"You're lucky." Jude took another napkin from the dispenser and dabbed at her mouth. "So where's the badge? You owe me the story."

Cara moaned. "What about the polite preliminaries? Are you sure you want to move to the subject of my bad career choices right away?"

"Absolutely," Jude said. "Why not? Other peoples' careers fascinate me."

Jude's no-nonsense attitude wasn't quite what Cara had expected. She was friendly and obviously at ease, but she didn't seem quite as accessible as she had the first time, at least not the way she was after they kissed. Maybe *that* Jude needed to be coaxed out first. And she wasn't sure she was up to the task. She wasn't sure she was up to any task other than being physically appealing.

"It's not really a story," she said, wiggling in her chair. "I quit, that's pretty much all there is to it. It wasn't for me." She curled some spaghetti round her fork. "I'd rather talk about your career choices."

Jude raised her eyebrows. "You know all about those already."

"The Santa gig?"

"Oh, that," Jude said. "I like to do one thing each year, incognito, that gives me a chance to meet my readers outside the obvious places like children's book stores and libraries. Last year I was a clown at a county fair, somewhere in…" She thought long and hard. "I'd like to say it was…Groningen?"

Cara nodded. "That's not impossible. Was it very flat, very windy, and very grey? And was it full of grassland and tractors that were stuck in the mud; and did you not understand a word anybody was saying?"

Jude laughed out loud. "Spot-on."

"Then it was probably Groningen."

"So this year, I chose to stay a little closer to home. And I definitely wanted my gig to have something to do with Christmas. I know that your Father Christmas is a pale version of ours, but I thought I might do my bit in bringing him to life for the little ones."

"Wow," said Cara. "There's no doubt that kids are definitely your thing."

Jude shrugged. "I guess so. Meeting my audience is an essential part of what I do, but it's not just work, it's something I really enjoy."

Yikes, Cara thought. She has the right answer to just about everything. She took a sip of her wine, her heart sinking as she realized, in a split second, that if she didn't come up with an inspiring story of perseverance and commitment of her own, this might very well be not only the first but also the last meal they'd share together.

"And they really enjoy seeing Bunny," Jude said. "You were *very* good at playing her, by the way. I was impressed with your magnificent improv. I was actually thinking of hiring you full time."

Cara smiled. "I'm definitely going to give that offer some thought." She moved her glass across the table, leaving wet stains on the wooden top. "Have you ever wanted any of your own? I mean kids?"

Jude took her time answering, which made Cara fear that her question was either inappropriate or painful. She cursed her lack of discretion, which tended to rear its head just when it mattered the most. And to think that her very own sister had been trying unsuccessfully to have a baby for longer than any of them cared to remember. Cara had sat with Inge countless times and shared her despair when yet another month passed by, when yet another period came. And the clock was ticking.

"I'm sorry," she said, "I tend to—"

"No, it's okay," said Jude. "I just...why would you think I don't have any of my own already?"

Cara let go of her glass. "Do you?"

Jude nodded.

Cara didn't know what to say. Somehow, she had never considered that Jude might be a mother. Now that it turned out she was, her situation suddenly became a whole lot more complicated. Was there…another mother? A father? Was Jude's lifetime partner still a force to be reckoned with, somewhere in the background? Had their breakup been temporary? And if there was a chance she'd patch things up with Laurie, would she have moved halfway across the world and gone on a date with someone new? Someone she had wanted to make out with so badly she had done so in public?

"Did I shock you?" Jude asked. She reached across the table and lightly touched Cara's arm. Cara's skin seemed to sparkle at the touch, but she couldn't concentrate on enjoying it. All this new information was just too distracting.

"No, no," she said. "I was just…wondering about a few things."

Jude pulled her hand back. "Tell me what they are, okay? You can ask me anything."

"Okay," Cara said, "I'll be perfectly honest."

Jude nodded.

"I'm beginning to wonder what we're doing here. Your signals are a little mixed. You have children, apparently. And an ex-partner, who is a woman. Were you raising a family with this Laurie? Or were you…with a man when you had them? Is there a chance you'll patch things up with someone? Are you moving back to California? Were we just…having a bit of fun the other night?" She shrugged. "Not that there's anything wrong with having fun. I just like to know where I stand. Or…"

Her voice trailed off as it dawned on her how presumptuous she must sound to someone who had no intention of taking this thing any further. She may very well have just set herself up to be brutally rejected.

"I'm single," Jude said. She held up her hands—no ring. "Have been for some time now. I'm definitely not going to patch things up with anyone. And I'm definitely gay." Her foot nudged Cara's under the table, an innocent way of establishing closeness. "I'll tell you the story if you like."

Cara nodded. "Please, do."

Jude's posture changed. She put her elbows on the table and leaned over confidentially, as if she were about to reveal a great secret. "I've known since I was a kid." She paused, staring out the window at the traffic in the street, while she doubtlessly remembered the first time she had understood that she wasn't like the other girls.

"Many gay people say that they always knew there was something different about them, but I didn't feel different at all, just gay. Or, for lack of a better term, boyish."

Cara smiled. Jude didn't seem very boyish now. Not that she would have minded—she wasn't exactly opposed to a subtle hint of butchness in the women she dated.

"I stunned a gathering of family and friends by coming out at my sweet sixteen party." Jude produced an evil grin. "It was awesome. All those people, huddled together in the kitchen of our Wisconsin farm, who had somehow managed to hold on to their 1950s values all through the decades—who maintained that masturbation would blind you and that womens' right to vote would be the country's undoing—were suddenly faced with the horror of a happily, and openly, gay daughter, granddaughter, and friend. It was the most confusing day in all of their lives."

"That was very brave of you," Cara said.

Jude shook her head. "It didn't feel that way at all. I simply felt that I had a right to live my life as proudly as any of them."

"So what happened after you came out? Did the sexy farm girls stop churning butter and turn their attention to you?" Cara giggled. "Hot summer nights in the haystack?"

Her mind produced an unexpectedly vivid image of such a scene, a little raunchy but not altogether unpleasant, that she was happy to keep to herself.

"Quite the contrary." Jude's voice dropped. She sounded sad and Cara pushed the budding fantasy out of her head.

Jude shrugged. "They didn't want anything to do with me. And if they did, their parents wouldn't allow them to. I was very young and I grew up in a traditional community. Kids didn't really tend to stand up to their parents. There were shared morals and values, nothing much seemed to change from one generation to the next. There was little acceptance of anything new or different."

Cara nodded sadly. Wasn't this a story that was familiar to far too many gay people?

"I became quite lonely," Jude said. "An outcast almost. My family accepted me as long as I didn't talk about girls, and I gradually came to realize how clueless they actually were. They were truly incapable of understanding that being gay is as real and permanent a sexual orientation as being straight—that it's not a temporary delusion, or a response to a bad experience, or a way to act out. So, they kept setting me up with the boys from the neighboring farms, convinced that I was bound to fall for one of them eventually, forget all this craziness, as they called it, and get married already. I couldn't stand it in the end, I was desperate to get away. So, as soon as I was eighteen, I moved to Los Angeles."

"And?"

"Let's just say I absolutely made up for lost time." Responding to Jude's impish smile, Cara made a mental note to ask her, at a more appropriate time, about details as to how and with whom she'd made up for lost time. She was a sucker for a good bedtime story.

"Are you still seeing your parents?"

"My father died of a massive heart attack, three years ago," Jude said. "I see my mother maybe three or four times a year. We never did talk about my orientation. They never asked if I was seeing anyone. When I got pregnant they seemed to assume I had chosen to be a single parent. Which happened to be true. I always suspected them of having made up a story to tell their friends—that my husband had left me, or died. But they were happy with my success and proud to be grandparents. I guess that was enough for me." She shrugged. "As you get older, you learn to choose your battles. Don't you think? And you tend to reconcile yourself to things that can't be changed. I miss my dad, but I'm glad I still have my mom, and I like spending time with her. I think she understands me better now, although she never says so. I only took Laurie out to the farm once; introducing her as a friend and as my illustrator, which she was. I'm sure my mom knew what was going on, but she never said anything and neither did I. I guess that over the years we learned to both give a little, meeting somewhere in the middle."

Cara nodded, realizing it wouldn't hurt if she were a little more forgiving herself. "Now," she said, "about your kids."

"I have one," Jude said. "Zoe. She's five." She shook her head. "But this is beginning to feel like an interview." She pushed the plate with the leftover lasagna across the table and picked up the bottle of house wine, which was empty. "Let's have a little more wine, okay?" she said. "And talk about you."

After the waiter had brought them both a glass of Chardonnay, Cara was wondering what she might reveal about herself that would make her seem even remotely as interesting as Jude. The impressive coming-out story, the brave move to such a different world, the child, the career, the fame—it was all a little intimidating. Was she really going to tell Jude the truth about herself? About how she had lost the badge? And how she'd become a pizza delivery girl instead? The story of how things had gone bad with Kelly, not to mention the string of girlfriends before her? How could she be honest about the lack of direction in her life now that she knew that Jude was a mother, that she had gone through the ordeal of losing a parent, that she had carefully planned her life and career, that she was wise and forgiving? Did she have any flaws at all? It was all so fucking serious! At the same time, the coming-out story had brought confusing new emotions—a tinge of pity, oddly arousing, and something that was, probably, plain old insecurity. She wasn't sure how she'd react if Jude decided to join the ranks of the people who tended to give her unsolicited advice, half-condescending, half-concerned, about how to get her act together.

"There's not that much to tell," she said. "I was actually interested in how you became a writer."

"I'll tell you some other time, okay? I'm sure there's plenty to say about you."

This annoyed Cara no end. Was it Jude's fame that made her think she knew Cara better than she knew herself? If she said there wasn't much to tell, then surely there wasn't. How could Jude deny that without knowing anything about her?

"I do believe I know myself a little better than you do," she scoffed.

Her angry voice seemed to startle Jude. She sat up and straightened her back, resting her hands in her lap.

"I'm sorry," Cara said. "I didn't mean to blow up like that." She was struggling to keep them on track here—to stop the whole night from turning sour.

"I'm obviously striking a sensitive chord," Jude said. "What's the matter? Don't you like talking about yourself?"

"Sure I do." Cara nodded. "It's just that my story seems a little embarrassing compared to yours. I'm not a great fan of planning or structure in my life. I don't like to be tied down or to commit to anything long term, apart from college, which was an incredibly inspirational time for me. After that, I watched people settle. Not just settle *down,* but settle. Personally, I've always been more interested in temporary projects than in building a career in one field. It's important to me to keep my options open. Not everybody understands or accepts that."

She took a deep breath, as it dawned on her how lame it all sounded. Was that even true? Was she really keeping her options open? Was she really interested in short term projects? Or was she trying to present herself as a nonconformist to impress Jude? She pushed a sudden sense of self-loathing away. This was hardly the time for soul searching.

"And since your resume is a little overwhelming…" Her voice trailed off. She didn't need to finish her sentence to make her point.

Jude took a sip of wine and leaned forward again, trying to bridge the gap between them. "I assure you, I won't think any less of you for not having a career. I wasn't expecting you to be just like me, or to meet some kind of requirement. Hell, I was just asking about your life. About you."

"Okay," Cara said, realizing she'd have to come clean eventually anyway. "The thing is, I deliver pizzas for Cara Mia."

Jude produced a wide grin. "So, at the bookstore, you were there in a professional capacity?"

"Not really," Cara said. "But anyway, I know you'll wonder what kind of job delivering pizzas is for a grown woman—"

"Hey!" Jude frowned. "Stop jumping to conclusions here, okay? I wasn't wondering that at all. Isn't being a grown woman all about deciding for yourself how you want to pay the bills?"

"It's not something I'm necessarily proud of," Cara said.

"But it's not something you're necessarily ashamed of either, right?"

Cara shook her head. "I guess not." She considered telling Jude that delivering pizza's was actually a study of the human condition; but she realized, in time, how hopelessly pedantic that would sound. Being pedantic was bad enough when there was a reason to be—it was an absolute turnoff when it was used to distract people from one's incompetence.

"It's great to see people find something they're passionate about," said Jude. "Doesn't really matter what it is—it can be anything from politics to stamp collecting. There's nothing as wonderful as doing something that makes your heart sing."

Cara chuckled. "I wouldn't go as far as to say that delivering pizza's makes my heart sing. But I guess I do okay. Being an artist is a different ball game, though. It must be awesome being a writer."

Jude nodded. "In all honesty, I'm struggling a little right now; but it's always been the most rewarding and utterly satisfying thing in the world to me."

"I feel a little intimidated," Cara confessed.

Jude shrugged. "Believe me, there's no need to be. Why would you?"

"Why would I…" Cara said, "…let's see. Could it be because I'm sitting here with Jude Donovan—gorgeous, famous, big shot writer? And could it be that I'm a little insecure because I have twenty dollars in the bank, a crappy job, a complete lack of ambition, and a secret addiction to romance novels while everybody thinks I spend my evenings studying the classics? I have no goals, no prospects, and I'm not going anywhere." She put her finger in the air, smirking. "Mind you, this is what my family says about me."

Jude picked up her napkin and held it in front of her face. Cara thought for a moment that she had burst into tears, but when Jude removed the napkin she realized that she was actually laughing.

Cara looked at her, her eyes cold. "Does my plight amuse you?"

"A little," Jude said. "Want to hear my plight? I'm being sued by some illiterate scumbag who says I stole his rabbit idea. I'm suffering from acute writer's block. My ex-wife is stalking me. I have PMS that's so impressive it's up for an award, and my kid is the first one to hit puberty at the tender age of five. All she does is scream at me and embarrass me in front of strangers." She smiled sweetly. "Plight schmight." she said. "But on a different note, did I just…hear you say… that I'm a *gorgeous,* famous, big shot writer?"

Cara pretended to think long and hard. "Nah," she said finally. "I really don't recall that I did. You must have heard wrong."

Jude was laughing out loud now. "You are a horrible woman," she said. "Hot. But horrible."

Cara raised her glass. "Right back at you."

The magic was back.

Chapter 6

"SO WHERE IS SHE NOW?" Cara said as they were leaving the restaurant. "Zoe, I mean."

"She's at a friend's house. My friend, not hers." Jude checked her watch. "She'll be sound asleep by now."

"Does that mean you have some sort of curfew?"

"No. Not really."

"What does that mean, not really? Either you do or you don't."

"It means," said Jude, buttoning up her elegant, long winter coat, "that I'm free as a bird. But that saying so seemed a little presumptuous."

"Ha!" Cara said. "Not at all." She wasn't about to let Jude get coy. "Let's get some fresh air, okay? Let's see what's going on at Dam Square. And then maybe we can catch the metro and have a little nightcap at my place."

Jude nodded. "A nightcap is fine. As long as it's not a euphemism for something else."

"O...kay." Cara wondered if that particular invitation was ever *not* a euphemism for something else.

"I mean, we can't have sex or anything," Jude said, out of the blue. She followed Cara down the street. "This is only our second date. And I'm not sure the first one even counts."

Cara was almost amused that Jude would bring this up quite so unceremoniously. It was unromantic, but strangely endearing. Cara felt more connected to Jude than she had the entire evening.

She shoved Jude with her elbow. "Who says you can't have sex on a second date? The Wisconsin moralists who corrupted you?"

Jude shook her head. "Anybody respectable."

"Well," said Cara. "They're wrong. Or maybe they're not, but who wants to be respectable anyway?"

"I do," Jude said. "And so do you. You're *so* not the stud you like to think you are."

"Who told you something so horrible about me?" Cara stared at her, eyes wide, pretending to be outraged. "Well? Did you Google me?"

Jude laughed. "No. I simply observed you trying to hide your pristine side. Unsuccessfully, I might add." She paused to wait until a party of loudly debating men in pinstriped suits had passed them. "You Googled *me* though."

"Who told you that?" Cara kicked an empty soda can along the cobblestones—the sound of late night hopes and doubts. It clanged against a streetlight, then lay still.

"You did."

"Right," Cara admitted. "I did. But you're a public figure. You have your own website."

"Which gives you an unfair advantage."

"Not at all." Cara shook her head. "It didn't tell me any of the things I wanted to know."

"Really?" Jude said. "Like what?"

Cara chose not to answer that. For now.

When they arrived at Dam Square, it was just after ten p.m., but it was still jam-packed with people. Not to mention pigeons.

"Ah," Jude said, staring at the beautifully illuminated façade of De Bijenkorf, "that's where it all started."

Cara thought back to all the times she'd made a fool of herself trying to find Jude. She'd never told her, and she wasn't about to do so now.

"Who knew," she said, "that we'd be standing here, only months later, voluntarily. And in peace." She smiled. "With actual fond memories of that day."

"Actually, I knew," Jude said. "Call me crazy, but I was always convinced we'd meet again some day."

Cara couldn't tell whether she meant it or not. They hadn't talked much about life and destiny. Maybe Jude was one of those people who thought that everything is connected, that everything happens for a reason.

"When I first came out here," Jude said, "I was all about the tourist attractions." She pointed to the back of the square, where the red-light district was. "I went there. And then I realized when I was there that it depressed me."

"It can be a little much to take in, this city," Cara said. "Sometimes, it's better to have a local as your guide."

Jude nodded. "I never went back. But this is a great spot. I want to read to the kids in this very square some time, in the open air—just like the other street artists. Wouldn't that be great? There's so much history here—the Royal Palace, the New Church, the National Monument." She pointed to the obelisk-shaped concrete pillar. "Even if it is a little phallic for my taste."

"Phallicism is in the eye of the beholder," Cara said. "Sometimes, a cigar is just a cigar."

Jude did what she'd done earlier, after their kiss on the bridge—she put her arm around Cara and pulled her close. It made Cara feel wonderful when she did that. It was intimate and yet innocent, it forged a bond between them. It made her want to tell her everything, to be herself without reservation.

"I couldn't believe how small everything is here," Jude said. "All these tiny streets and tiny passages and tiny houses—a tiny country inhabited by freakishly tall people."

"I'm not surprised you feel that way," Cara said, "coming from a country where the food comes in buckets and the drinks in drums."

Jude pulled her arm back and bumped her hip against Cara's. "O my God!" she said. "I've offended you." She laughed. "You're a closeted patriot."

"Don't call me that." Cara pretended to pout. "That's an insult to people like me."

Jude leaned over and kissed her on the cheek.

For some reason, Cara felt a sudden surge of happiness course through her. It was so strong that it made her dizzy.

"Did you know," she said, "that this very place was once the hippie capital of the country? Maybe even of the whole of Europe?"

Cara pictured the square in her mind the way she'd seen in old photographs.

She sighed. "I wish I could have been here back then, in the sixties. It was *the* place for sit-ins, sleep-ins, and every kind of peaceful, pot-induced protest against the established order you could think of. If I'd been around then, I would *definitely* have been a part of that. It must have been such a great time to be alive."

Jude looked at her lovingly. Her eyes were dark, her skin seemed to glow. "I think I'm ready for that nightcap now," she said.

Cara nodded. "Would you prefer the buzzing nightlife at Leidseplein Square, or the quiet splendor of my apartment?"

Jude grinned. "The latter. Where's your car?"

"Don't have it here," Cara said. "Sorry. Parking is hell in the city. Which is why I cycle or take the metro."

Jude looked at her in amazement. "You've cycled in this city and lived to tell?"

"Sure," Cara said. "We have a special skill. But I took the metro in today."

"So lead on, then," Jude said. "Take us underground."

But as they headed for a metro station, Jude asked Cara if they could take a tram instead. There was nothing to see on the metro, she insisted, while traveling by tram was a wonderful way to be part of the hustle and bustle of the city from a safe distance.

"I'm in love with the sound of the tram bells," she said. "It's part of the music of Amsterdam."

Once in the tram, they sat side by side on the comfortable blue seats, looking out the window.

"This is cozy," Jude said, moving closer to Cara.

"I live in a very ugly apartment building," Cara said, out of the blue.

Jude giggled. "You sure know how to make a girl's head spin."

"Well," Cara said, "it's true. And I thought I might as well warn you now. I know that you dwellers of the canal belt don't really know how the other half lives."

"You could live in a tent for all I care," Jude said. She seemed to be in very high spirits now. It was as if their little falling out at the restaurant had cleared the air and given way to a feeling of trust and lightheartedness between them. Or maybe, Jude was simply an easygoing person. Cara wanted to pinch herself—an easygoing girlfriend, now *that* was a first. She scolded herself for thinking of Jude as her girlfriend. Too hard, too soon. Would she ever learn?

"What's that look?" Jude said.

Cara realized that Jude was staring at her and that she had a worried look in her face.

"Are you having second thoughts?" Jude asked. The tram made a stop and she laughed. "Please, don't make me get off here, in the..." she struggled to read the name on the display. "....Egidiusstraat." She puffed. "That doesn't really roll off the American tongue smoothly, does it?"

"I think you're a natural," Cara said. "I'd never have known you weren't a local. And I'm definitely not having second thoughts."

To emphasize how much she wasn't having second thoughts, she rested her hand on Jude's leg. Possessive? So what. She knew it was there, Jude knew it was there—hell, *everybody* knew it was there. And it felt so right.

When they got off the tram, Cara pointed to a block of flats down the street. "That's it," she said. "Are you coming?"

Jude followed her, staring at the building. "I don't see what's wrong with it," she said.

Cara shrugged. "My apartment is on the fifth floor. It would have had a great view if there was actually anything to see."

"You have a habit of talking down on things for no reason," Jude said.

The tiled hall was full of old bicycles. Stacks of envelopes were piled on top of the mailboxes on the wall. Cara saw Jude stare at them, eyebrows raised.

"Bills," she explained. "Friendly and slightly less friendly requests to pay for services rendered. I could have made a living as a process server and never left my own building."

"Interesting," Jude said as they stepped on the elevator. She pressed the button for the fifth floor and then nudged Cara. "You still owe me an answer to my question."

"What question?"

"The information you wanted that was missing from my website. We aim to inform, you know."

Cara swallowed. "I was just wondering…" she said.

"Yes?"

"How you sound…"

"How I sound?"

"When you…you know."

"Jesus," said Jude, putting her hand on the wall for support.

"Just to name something."

"Please, don't name anything else," Jude said, "or you'll make me faint."

"We can't have that." Cara grinned. "We're here, by the way."

The elevator doors slid open and they stepped out into a narrow lobby with five doors on either side. Cara opened her front door. It had a peephole.

"No cats?" Jude said, walking into the hall. She opened the door to a wonderfully spacious and bright living room and stepped inside.

"No cats," Cara said. "And no taste in interior design to speak of." She kicked off her shoes. "And I'm okay with that."

"What do you mean, no taste in interior design to speak of?" Jude was standing in the middle of the room, surveying it. "I never know how to respond to people's modesty." She unbuttoned her coat, took it off and hung it over a chair. "Am I supposed to contradict them, or to tell them that I too think they suck at whatever they claim to suck at."

Cara shrugged. "It wasn't my intention to be modest. It's just that most people who see my place for the first time tell me that walking in here is like walking into an anemic Ikea catalogue."

"Most people are full of it," Jude said. "What's wrong with buying furniture from a place that sells it? Who has time to scour the flea markets for hidden treasures and spend months fixing them up? I know I don't."

"Have a seat." Cara pointed to her comfortable grey couch.

Jude sat down. She took off her jacket and draped it neatly over the armrest. She made herself comfortable, sinking back into the cushions. "Maybe the place could do with a little more color," she said, looking around. "A couple of throw pillows and houseplants might liven it up. Other than that, I think it's quite tasteful. And I love your collection." She pointed to the wall-to-wall bookcase. "Who has real books anymore?"

"I'll give you a tour later," Cara said, walking into the kitchen. "What will you have?" She picked up a bottle from the cooking island and eyed it suspiciously. "This is empty, I'm afraid. Which leaves us with a choice of some leftover Tequila or..." She began to open and close cabinets doors "...as it turns out, some leftover Tequila."

"I'm not sure," Jude said. "I guess I'll go with the Tequila."

Cara nodded. "Excellent choice."

She poured the drinks, walked into the room, handed Jude a glass and sat next to her, close enough to ensure a subtle and seemingly undeliberate touching of thighs.

Jude looked at her glass doubtfully. "On second thought, I'm not sure how wise it is to drink this after all that wine. I'm not really used to so much alcohol."

"It'll go to your head." Cara sounded as if she couldn't wait for that to happen.

"So what exactly was the Tequila left over from? Did you have a bash?"

Cara laughed. "A bash? Hardly. I'm all work and no play, didn't you know?"

"Poor you." Jude turned toward her, breaking the contact between their thighs, but making up for it by staring into Cara's eyes and putting a hand on her knee. "Poor, beautiful Cara. No fun in your life, ever?"

Cara shook her head.

"Maybe we could…" Jude moved her hand up Cara's leg, slowly, from the knee to the thigh, and higher still, her thumb leading the way. Just as Cara was about to gasp, she stopped.

"Tease."

Jude smiled. "Good things come to those who wait."

"I've been wondering," Cara said, feeling a familiar tingle in the pit of her stomach, "about your necklace." She stretched out her hand and touched the delicate silver design, resting her fingers lightly on Jude's skin.

"Someone had it specially made for me," Jude said, "by a silversmith. It represents two things that are opposite to some, but not to me." She brought her own hand to the necklace, finding Cara's fingers there. "I stopped seeing the person who gave it to me, a long time ago, but it's still a reminder to me that such a thing is possible. To be united, and still, somehow, free."

Cara nodded.

"In my experience," Jude said, "it's pretty much impossible to have both." She shrugged. "I either wind up with someone who takes the freedom a little too far, or with someone who can't stand to be apart for ten minutes."

"I'm not so sure it's impossible to have both at all." Cara liked what she heard. "Anyway, it's beautiful." She let go of the necklace, but allowed her fingers to trail down, hiding them in the fabric of the shirt, until she felt them enveloped by soft, warm flesh.

Jude's breath hitched.

Cara wanted to put her glass on the table, but she knew that to do so, she must remove her hand.

It was a dilemma of sorts, that Jude watched her struggle with for a moment, the corners of her mouth curling up. "Let me help you," she said finally. "Something tells me you'll be needing both hands here." Her voice was low, like a purr. She took the glass and put it on the side table next to the couch. "You really didn't think this through, did you?" She shook her head. "Amateur."

"We'll see who's an amateur," Cara whispered as she started to unbutton Jude's blouse. Jude leaned over, looking for Cara's mouth, and she grabbed her wrists, keeping both their arms suspended in the air. Cara, frustrated though she was, tried to resign to her hands being tied. She concentrated, instead, on the kiss; gentle, lazy almost, similar to before, but without the urgency.

"There is a point of no return here, you know?" Jude's voice was muffled, her lips brushing Cara's.

"Reached and passed it," Cara whispered. As soon as she had her hands back, she continued unbuttoning Jude's blouse. Jude leaned back slightly, giving access, watching Cara's every move with interest. When Cara was done, she slid the soft fabric over Jude's shoulders. Drawing from rich experience in sliding women's blouses over their shoulders, Cara was surprised at how alarmingly intimate it was to see Jude like this. It was fairly innocent—it was nothing you couldn't see in dressing rooms, in swimming pools, at beaches. And still. It was as if there was an unusual intensity to it all—as if they had crossed a line that had very little to do with sex, but everything with connectedness, with trust. Cara shivered, not because she relished it, but because it startled her. She tried to restore the balance by upping the ante, running eager hands over Jude's shoulders and hooking her fingers beneath the bra straps.

Before she could drag them down, Jude moved out of reach of her hands. "Let's wait a second here, okay?"

Cara dropped her hands in her lap, ready to scream. "What's wrong? Please, don't tell me we're taking another rain check." She exhaled loudly. "There aren't enough cold showers in the world—"

"Don't worry. No rain check." Jude smiled. "I just thought that maybe…you know—is there a place where we'll be a little more comfortable? Like…a bed?"

Cara got up, holding out her hand to Jude as if she were asking her to dance.

Jude got up too, trying, for some reason, to readjust her blouse.

"Don't bother," Cara said. "There is a bed, and this..." she tugged at the shirt, "...is definitely coming off."

"Who's corrupting me now, huh?"

"I am." Cara practically dragged Jude down the hall. "It'll be my pleasure."

"Oh, and so you know," Jude said as they entered the bedroom, "I'm quiet."

Cara looked puzzled, as Jude's hands began to wander over her body, the fingertips as light as butterflies. Jude pulled Cara's shirt out of her jeans and over her head. She brought her hand to Cara's head and opened the clasp that was holding her hair up, watching it fall and running her hands through it. She grunted and buried her face in the wavy blond locks. Her gaze shifted, and she moved her hands to Cara's jeans. She opened the belt, the button, the zipper. The urgency was back—her motions growing impatient and determined.

"Quiet?" Cara loved the way Jude was all over her.

Jude stuck a teasing finger inside Cara's panties, making her gasp.

"When I...you know."

Cara unhooked Jude's bra, then her own. She filled her hands and marveled.

"That sounds like a challenge." Cara bent over and gently bit Jude's earlobe. Jude giggled, as she crouched down and began to tug at the denim of Cara's jeans with impatient fingers. Cara knew her panties would be next, and as she felt the fabric being slid down her legs, slowly exposing her, she was afraid she'd come before they even made it to the bed.

They woke up to a bright new day. No regrets, no doubts.

Cara was exhilarated to find that Jude didn't seem to feel the need to discuss the state of their relationship after 'you know, last night,' knowing all too well that the simplicity of sex on the night you had it tended to turn into the most complicated thing in the world in the cold light of day.

"I can't believe you told me you have no accomplishments." Jude's voice clinked like an ice cube in a glass.

"I can't believe you told me you were quiet." Cara smirked.

Jude rolled over, straddled Cara, and leaned forward to kiss her. "I guess your accomplishments and my volume are somehow connected. You are one talented woman, Cara Jong. Remind me to rewrite that resume for you, okay?"

It was going to be a great morning, one of the best Cara could remember.

Chapter 7

"I CAN'T BELIEVE YOU'RE DATING Jude Donovan," Myra said. "And she has a child! I never knew that. You're practically a mother yourself, now. Especially since there's no father."

"There is a father," Cara said.

"A gay friend donating his sperm in a turkey baster and then joining the foreign legion is hardly a father."

"He never joined the foreign legion," Cara said. "I don't even think the foreign legion exists anymore. He's doing volunteer work in Africa somewhere. And he didn't exactly donate his sperm *in* the turkey baster, he just—"

"Okay!" Myra pushed her hand in Cara's face. "We get it! Enough sperm talk. But really, I can't believe you're dating Jude Donovan." She nodded approvingly. "Well done."

"It's not really dating," Cara said. "It's...seeing. I'm seeing her."

"How is that different?" Myra rested her hand on her stomach. She was a little less bouncy, being in her third trimester.

Cara shrugged. "I don't want you guys to get all overboard here, the way you do."

"So what's she like?" Inge asked.

"She's amazing."

"How's the sex?"

Cara wasn't prepared for the question, nor for its impact. Vivid images of her night with Jude began to bombard her thoughts, and it was as if not nearly enough oxygen was making it to her head.

"I don't know," she said stoically, bluffing her way through it. "We're not in that place."

"That good, huh?" Inge patted her on the shoulder. "I'm impressed."

"Do they ask about me?"

Cara nodded. "All the time. They're desperate to meet you. I've been giving them updates ever since we met at the De Bijenkorf, when you were so horribly cruel to me. They know everything."

Jude stretched out her hands and put them on Cara's hips, pulling her closer. "Everything?" she said coyly. "They know *everything*?"

Cara leaned over and put her lips on Jude's ear. "Yes," she whispered, delighting at the goose bumps raising all over Jude's arms. "They told me to have my way with you any chance I get."

Jude writhed and giggled as the tip of Cara's tongue touched her ear. "Have your way with me? That's what they said? Exactly, what *is* your way?"

Cara pushed her down gently on the bed, and showed her. Twice.

"What's up?" Cara kept her phone between her chin and her shoulder, balancing her laptop in the air with one hand and an empty coffee cup with the other.

"Not much," Inge said. "I was just wondering how you're doing."

"Fine. You?" Cara put down the computer and the mug on the coffee table and fell down on the couch.

"Okay. So how's it going with Jude?"

"Pretty good."

"Come on, Cara, give me something here. Don't make me beg."

"If you must know, we went out last night. We had a beef croquette at Febo's. From the vending machine."

Inge gave a snort of disgust. "Febo's? Really? Why? Not that I'm not a fan, but isn't that a bit tacky for a date?"

"It's part of Jude's education in Dutch culture," Cara said. "Which is long overdue. She has managed to stay 100 percent American and that has to stop."

"So you spent the entire night at Febo's?"

"No, we went to the movies afterward."

"What did you see?"

"*The Hunger Games.*"

"Really? Isn't that for kids?"

"They call them young adults now."

"So? You don't qualify, no matter what they're called."

"The story appeals to all ages. I'm simply a fan."

"Jennifer Lawrence, huh?"

"What can I say? She *is* on fire."

"Cradle robber."

Cara laughed. "It's not just that, I really am a fan, although I do agree that the whole concept of children being forced to fight to the death is a little questionable, to say the least."

"Did you hold hands?"

"With Jude? No, we actually watched the movie. We didn't hold hands until afterward."

"You sound happy," Inge said approvingly on the other end of the line.

"It's pretty awesome, you know, going out with her." Cara got up, walked barefoot to the kitchen, opened the fridge and scanned the contents. She picked up a can of soda and walked back to the couch. She sat down, folding her legs beneath her in what Inge called 'that timeless way of hot blondes.'

The soda fizzled and liquid bubbled over, running down the side of the can and over her fingers. She brought her mouth to her hand and licked it off.

"What's that sound?" Inge asked suspiciously. "Is she there with you now?"

"No." Cara sighed. "Could you get your mind out of the gutter for one second?"

"Sorry. But go on. You were saying how great she is."

"And how great I am too," Cara said. "I'm so funny. And erudite. I draw from a secret source of knowledge and wit I never knew was there. I don't recognize myself when I'm with her. It's like...whoa; who is this wildly interesting person sitting across from Jude, with her playful banter and her titillating, but never vulgar, observations? Could it be *moi*? I swear to God, even my complexion has improved."

"Erudite?" Inge said, baffled.

"I was wondering about your writer's block. Your acute writer's block."

Jude stretched her long legs, ran a hand through her hair and sighed. "Again? Can't we talk about something else?"

"Why?" Cara eyed her innocently. She'd been treading carefully whenever any aspect of Jude's work came up, strangely intimidated to be so close to the actual creative process. She didn't want to take on the role of anybody 'in the business,' be it an agent, an interviewer, or even simply a fan. But she'd come to realize that she got it wrong. Being close to the creative process entitled her to ask questions an agent or interviewer might not. Except that now, there seemed to be no creative process to speak of.

Jude shrugged and closed the book she'd been reading. "What can I say? It's not exactly my favorite subject."

"But I want to know," Cara insisted. "Is it like some sudden, mysterious inability to express your inner thoughts, or is it more like...when a baker has baker's block?"

Jude shook her head and got up from her chair. The subject obviously made her too nervous to sit and answer difficult questions. She began to walk aimlessly across her living room, picking things up and putting them down again, rearranging pillows, collecting empty glasses and taking them to the kitchen.

"Baker's block?" she said when she walked back into the room. She sat down at the dinner table, wiping her hand across the top to remove invisible crumbs. She oozed unease whenever the subject of her not being able to write came up. "There's no such thing as baker's block. As far as I'm aware."

"Exactly," Cara said. "Nor is there plumber's block. Or trauma surgeon's block."

"Thank God for that," said Jude.

"Seems like you guys are the only ones affected by this strange affliction."

"What's your point?"

"Maybe," Cara said, bracing for impact, "you should simply sit down and get the job done."

Jude flashed her an angry frown. "Are you suggesting I'm *pretending* that I can't write right now? Do you think I *like* feeling like a dried up well?"

"Ugh," Cara said. "What a horrible image. You so don't resemble a dried up well." She smiled mischievously. "All your juices are running freely."

"Ew," said Jude.

"Why can't your creative juices run freely too?"

"It's not that simple," Jude said. "All professions have a certain degree of routine to them, no matter how complicated they are. All except the arts. An artist has to reinvent the world time after time."

"And there you go with a title," Cara said smugly. "Bunny reinvents the world time after time."

Jude shook her head. "I appreciate your attempt at humor, and I understand that the pressure I'm under is nothing compared to yours or anyone else's in the hamburger flipping or pizza delivering business, but this is no laughing matter to me."

"Ouch," Cara said. "What brought this on?"

Jude muttered a vague apology.

"I want to help, you know?" Cara said finally. "Maybe we could try together."

"Really?"

Cara nodded.

"I have the feeling you're not taking this seriously. That you think anybody could do it," Jude said.

"I don't—"

"Maybe you believe, like so many, that children's book writers are people who started out writing for adults but couldn't cut it."

"I don't know," Cara said. "I never really thought about that."

"Children's literature is in a league of its own," Jude said, raising her voice. "It has its own challenges and demands, especially for us, who write for the very young."

Cara nodded hesitantly.

"I really don't care for your condescending nod! Don't you believe me?"

"I'm sorry," Cara said. "I really know very little about this." She took a second to find the right words. "In all honesty, I'd be inclined to say that it's easier to write *Bunny Has a Boo-Boo* than to write *Mrs. Dalloway*." She shrugged. "On the other hand, Woolf had a bit of a boo-boo of her own. If you're trying to convey roughly the same emotions she did; I'm sure that doing so for an audience with a twenty-word vocabulary is no easy feat." She cocked her head and looked at Jude pleadingly. "Let's not fight about this, okay? You know I love your work. And your commitment to your readers. Let me be a part of this. Show me what you have."

Jude reached into her purse and pulled out a black leather notebook. "Just a couple of lines so far," she said, leafing through the pages. 'Bunny was a little sad. A tear was rolling down her cheek.'" She hung her head. "Yes, it's embarrassing, I know."

Cara couldn't read the line from where she was sitting, but she did see that most of the page was filled with doodles, in red ink, making it look like someone had been bleeding on it.

"So what's troubling her?" Cara said. "I mean Bunny. Why is she sad?"

"You know about the last volume, right? *Bunny Finds a Friend*?"

Cara nodded. She had, by now, read the entire series.

"Well, this time, she loses one."

"To what?" Cara pulled a face, hoping this wouldn't be the volume that introduced the toddler fans to the horrors of divorce or death.

"A move," Jude said.

"Not a move to…heaven?"

"No, no. Oregon."

Cara chuckled. "I see. Hell."

Jude eyed her with an amused expression on her face. "Bad experience in Oregon?"

"Not at all," Cara said, "I've never even been there. In my mind it's a cold and empty place."

"The focus is on introducing the concept of loss, and how to deal with that."

"I see." Cara smiled. "It's not about Oregon at all."

Jude got up and walked across the room to Cara's chair. She sat down on her lap, resting her head in the hollow of Cara's neck. Cara put her arm around her and kissed the top of her head. A confused sensation, something that was halfway between sadness and bliss crept up on her out of nowhere.

They sat like that for a while; neither of them spoke.

"Sometimes," Jude said finally, "I know, in my heart, that I can do this really great thing, you know? That I can rise above myself. And then I'm almost afraid to start writing, because I know that as soon as I touch it, it might break."

She lifted her head and locked eyes with Cara. She opened the top buttons of Cara's shirt with one hand, parted the lapels with an impatient tug, and moved her hand there.

"Have you ever felt that way about anything, Ms. Jong?"

Cara sucked in a deep breath. "No," she whispered. "I can't say that I have."

Chapter 8

"ARE YOU THE SORT OF person who tends to wonder where things are going?"

"Things? What things?"

"I mean, in relationships."

"Oh, that." Cara shrugged as if the subject was of no particular interest to her, but she couldn't help but stiffen slightly. She knew, without even looking at her, that Jude was holding her breath, waiting for the answer with well concealed anxiety. In the silence that followed, it was as if Cara could hear both their hearts beat. "Not particularly."

She brought Jude's hand to her face and kissed the inside of the wrist, pressing her lips to the delicate network of bluish veins. Her mind went back to Tanja, one of the first girls she had ever slept with, who would pride her on finding erogenous zones that nobody had found before. Cara smiled as she recalled that she, in turn, would tell Tanja that people should know better than to always look in the obvious places.

"Why?" Jude said.

Cara hesitated. "Let's just say that I've learned to take things one day at a time, and to shy away from making promises I can't keep."

She hated herself as soon as she'd said the words. She let go of Jude's hand. How could she be the sort of person who kisses someone's wrist, while at the same time warning her that she shouldn't read too much into it. The words made her feel unworthy of Jude's time, let alone of her love. She sighed, blowing a strand of hair from her forehead. Couldn't this, for once in her life, be easy?

She trailed behind, picking up a soda can and throwing it in a recycling bin. She wanted to watch Jude as she walked ahead—her slender body in the black chiffon blouse, her long legs in a pair of high-waisted grey pants. Jude had taken off her jacket and was holding it in her right hand, where it dangled by her side, almost, but not quite, touching the ground.

Jude was always a study in contradiction. There was something languid and yet determined about the way she moved. She was a person who knew where she was going, but who was willing to take her time getting there. She oozed strength and confidence in such a natural way, that the touch of vulnerability that was also there seemed to enhance rather than contradict it. There was something pure about her that Cara had initially mistaken for the opposite—a public person's studied coyness. She had soon realized that it was genuine, and probably part of what made Jude successful. In a sense, she was the most laid-back person Cara had ever known. Which was another contradiction, at least to Cara. How was Jude able to combine that attitude with a life where she had so many obligations to fulfill, people to placate, deadlines to make?

Jude's head was surrounded by a shimmering aureole where the light caught her hair. She had rolled her shirt sleeves up to the elbows, revealing the smooth, olive skin of her forearms; a large, white watch dangling loosely on her right wrist, and a crochet beaded bracelet—a Mother's Day present from Zoe—on the left. Cara realized, observing her, that Jude was the sort of person she might have walked up to if she had happened to meet her in the street somewhere, like in a movie, where someone sees their own destiny reflected in a stranger's eyes. She reminded herself that she didn't believe in destiny, and she reminded herself also of that strange contradiction, that the more spiritual one's feelings seem, the more mundane they are.

Jude turned around to see what was keeping her, standing still until Cara caught up with her.

"How did you learn that?"

"What?" Cara asked absentmindedly.

"To take things one day at a time and to avoid making promises?"

"It sounds like a cliché," Cara said, "and I guess it is, but I've realized that the way I feel about someone tends to change over time. Time is like a storm—it sweeps over the land and mows the prettiest flowers down." She looked at Jude apologetically. "No offense."

"None taken," said Jude.

Cara breathed a sigh of relief. It was wonderful, and unprecedented, how openly and respectfully they were able to talk about subjects as sensitive as this one.

"But why do you ask?" she said. "Should we talk about where our thing is going? Because contrary to popular belief, this is not necessarily a conversation I'm unwilling to have."

She looked around, enjoying the hustle and bustle at one of her favorite spots in the city, Vondelpark. She loved the place in every season, because even though it was always crowded, nobody ever got in her way. There was plenty of room for everyone to enjoy it. Taking a stroll down the paths in the hilly grassland with its abundance of trees and meandering streams, followed by having a cup of coffee on the upper terrace of the café, would always have a wonderfully relaxing effect on her.

Vondelpark was a two-kilometer-long park in Amsterdam-Zuid, but it stretched all the way to Amsterdam-West. It was designed according to the English landscape style—full of winding paths and rose gardens. It had a teahouse, it had restaurants and bars—it even had an open air theatre where performances were held during the summer months.

There were a lot of dogs today, taking out their owners. And a lot of teenagers, walking hand in hand. A middle-aged couple was having a picnic on the grass; sitting close together on a quilt, they fed each other sandwiches and fruit. Some kids were playing soccer on one of the fields. There were scores of joggers and skaters. The sun warmed her face, and Cara felt a rush of happiness. She was about to talk about the state of her relationship, and she stood firmly, confidently.

"I don't know." Jude looked around. She spread her arms as if she were trying to hug the day, the park. "It seems like a typical afternoon to talk about plans, somehow. Maybe it's the spring. Maybe it's a nesting thing."

It was a cool but sunny day with a fresh breeze blowing in. It was the first time they were out in public in the daytime. Jude smiled. "It's such a peaceful, let's-throw-caution-to-the-wind-and-buy-rings day." She pressed a hand to her mouth, shocked. "Does this freak you out?"

Cara laughed. "No," she said, "it doesn't. We're both honest, and that's the most important thing. In fact, I threw a soda can in a recycling bin that had a perfectly good ring on it not two minutes ago. That could have been yours. If only I'd known." She threw her arm around Jude possessively and kissed her, causing a young boy on a bicycle, who was passing them, to take an unexpected detour and land in the grass next to his bike. He got up quickly, rubbed his knees, stuck out his tongue to them, and sped off.

"We'd definitely be buying rings if this were a movie." Jude stared off into space, a dreamy expression on her face. "This could be the opening shot. Without the young homophobe, of course." She pointed to the sky. "Picture a bright, clear, breezy day. Picture two people, making plans, totally oblivious to the fact that plans tend to get derailed."

"Okay," Cara said. "What exactly does the script prescribe we do?"

"That would depend on the genre."

"Let's say we're in a romantic comedy."

Jude took Cara's hand and led her to a bench where she sat down. "Well," she said, "in a romantic comedy, I would tell you that nobody has ever made me feel the way you do, and then I would give you a chaste kiss and present you with a key to my apartment." She shrugged. "To emphasize my commitment to you, I would probably have had a keychain made, depicting something you were passionate about." She leaned forward, resting her elbows on her knees. "Basset hounds. Kites. Captain Janeway in her spandex Starfleet uniform."

Cara sat down next to her and looked up at the puffy clouds in the clear blue sky, wondering what magical things might happen if Jude used her impressive powers of imagination to write adult literature. The thought almost made her dizzy. Or maybe it was the vastness of the sky that did that.

"So I suppose," Cara said, "that the key to your apartment would be symbolizing the key to your heart." She rested her hand on Jude's back. The warmth of her skin radiated through the thin fabric of her shirt and it made Cara feel oddly possessive.

Jude nodded. "Of course, there would have to be some kind of conflict, or problem, otherwise there's no story. Maybe you could get hit by a car and spend a year in a coma."

"And then I'd wake up unable to move anything but my left eyebrow," Cara said with drama in her voice, "forced to watch you make out with some hot writer chick while you sit at my bedside, pretending to care, until you decide to have mercy on me and pull the plug."

Jude eyed her critically. "You don't really understand the romantic comedy, do you?"

Cara smiled. "What if it were a costume drama?"

"I don't know," Jude said, "I don't watch costume dramas. I guess it would be the same, only the key would be to a castle, and we'd be sitting here with our servants, sweating in twenty layers of velvet and wool and rusty chastity belts."

"That we probably wouldn't have the key to," said Cara. "Ugh. So what if it were a thriller?"

Jude sat up and straightened her back. Cara thought she saw a glimmer of irritation zipping across her face, but she wasn't sure.

"If it were a thriller we'd find a dead body floating in the pond, and it were sci-fi we'd be abducted by aliens, and if it were a horror movie there'd be a guy with a chainsaw waiting for us in the bushes."

Jude got up, brushing something invisible off her shirt. "The thing is," she said, "I sort of have the feeling that you're missing the point here." She began to walk away. Cara wasn't sure if she was offended or simply disappointed. Or neither.

"I'm not." Cara rose abruptly and followed her. "Tell me what it is you want to say. Or ask."

"Look." Jude was standing still. "I'm not asking for a ring here. Or a promise."

Cara just stood there, waiting.

Jude shrugged. "I'm not really asking for anything."

"You're not?"

"I only know what I feel."

Cara threw caution to the wind, sick of having to imagine the other person's response to everything, and sick of abiding by the codes that accompanied every fucking step in a relationship, until you were finally hooked and all codes flew out the window. The only right way to go here was to be honest. Painfully and completely honest. She reached for Jude's hand.

"Listen, Jude," she said. "I'm not sure I should tell you this, and I'm honestly not asking for validation, but I have *nothing* to offer you."

Jude held her gaze. "Don't you get it?" she said. She brought her free hand to Cara's face and tucked a few loose strands of blond hair behind her ear. "It's you, Cara," she said simply. "You're the one. I had to travel halfway across the world to find you. And now that I did, there's no way I'm letting you go, no matter how much you put yourself down."

☽ ☾ �}

"What can one do on a rainy night like this?" Cara did a drumroll on the dinner table.

Jude, who turned out to be a horrible cook, had made a salad, or rather, she had bought a salad, in a plastic container, and divided it onto two plates. That wasn't even the worst meal she'd ever served. She knew her wine, though, which made up for a lot.

The apartment was quiet—Zoe was having a sleepover at a friend's house. They'd stayed in all day. Jude had tried to write; Cara was rereading *The Well of Loneliness*, an old classic that she had always enjoyed, despite the review that said, "This book will make you wish you were dead."

Outside, a storm was raging.

"I should have added something," Jude mused, holding her glass by the stem and gently twirling it. "Chicken. Or maybe pasta." She looked doubtful. "Right? The salad alone was not a balanced meal."

"It was," Cara assured her. "It's what people call a light dinner. And it's a proven fact that people who eat fewer calories live longer."

"You're just saying that," said Jude. "Because you don't want to aggravate me."

"On the contrary. I love aggravating you."

"But you love something else more." Jude's voice was like treacle—slow, sweet, and thick. Cara knew that voice, and she felt her body respond to it immediately.

"I have no idea what you're talking about."

Jude got up and walked around the table. "I'm hungry," she said. Her eyes were dark, shining like stars in the night sky. "For you. For your deliciousness."

A bolt of lightning shot across the sky, bathing them in an eerie, white light.

"Damn paparazzi," Cara whispered, stretching out her arms.

Jude laughed as she straddled Cara. "You're so weird," she said. She lost the smile and locked her gaze with Cara's. "There's something about you, did you know that?"

Before Cara could answer, Jude growled, the sound mirrored by a drawn-out rumble of thunder outside. Jude ran her hands across Cara's scalp, tugging her head back, and initiated a kiss, heated and impatient. Her tongue touched Cara's at the exact moment the long awaited clash of thunder and lightning split the sky in two.

Chapter 9

CARA MET ZOE ON A Saturday in early April. The wonderfully sunny spring day was drawing to a close. The evening was warm, enticing, and full of promise. If ever there was love in the air, it had to be now. April, she thought, was anything *but* the cruelest month. She was lightheaded and dizzyingly in love when she went over to Jude's apartment to pick her up for a night on the town. She knew, somehow, that they were about to share the most romantic night ever. She had cleaned and tidied her apartment with great care, pulling out all the stops when turning her bedroom into a romantic hideaway. There were fresh flowers on the dresser. There was champagne in a cooler. There were rose petals on the bed. There was a CD with late night jazz in the stereo. The thrill of anticipation made her shiver.

Jude seemed a little flushed and nervous when she opened the door. And not in a good way. The sitter was there, but Zoe, who was supposed to be asleep, was anything but. She was feverishly running around the living room, clutching a pink elephant under her arm.

"Look," Cara said, "there's a pink elephant in the room." She smiled at the girl, who looked adorable, wearing Hello Kitty pajamas and a pair of fuzzy slippers on her little feet.

Cara reached out her hand to the child. She was going to do this right. She and Zoe would be as close as two coats of paint in no time. What was the secret again? Respect, right. She remembered what Jude had told her at the bookstore. Respect them, and they will respond in turn.

But Zoe took one look at Cara, and her expression changed dramatically. This sweet kid flashed her an evil grin and began to holler.

"Mommy!" she cried. "I feel sick!"

Jude came storming down the hall. "I'm right here. What's wrong? You weren't sick two minutes ago."

"I want Mommy!" Zoe hollered again.

"Shush," Jude said. She sat down and took the child on her lap. "I'm here!"

"No!" Zoe screamed. "I want Mommy Laurie!"

Jude's face turned to ice. Cara could tell she needed a second to recover. Then she shook her head. "Aw, honey," she said. "Mommy Laurie's not here right now, you know that. She's at the ranch, remember?"

Zoe managed to produce a couple of tears and wrapped her arms more tightly around her mother's neck. She sniffed.

"Sweetie, sweetie," Jude said, patting her back, "I promise we'll go see Mommy Laurie soon, okay?"

And then something strange happened. Zoe, her chin resting on Jude's shoulder, focused her eyes on Cara. When she did, her mouth curled up in what Cara could only call a vindictive smile. She couldn't believe the little manipulator. Anyone could tell she was faking it. Anyone but Jude.

"Because she can!" Jude spit out the words. "Because making my life miserable is her new goal in life!" She shook her head. "I can't believe I was ever stupid enough to get involved with this woman. Let alone marry her." She was pacing the floor of her apartment, picking up throw pillows and hurling them across the room. Jude was one of those people who rarely expressed rage, and when she did, it was always contained enough to never actually break something valuable.

Cara rested a hand on her shoulder, trying to calm her down. It seemed like all they were doing these days was fighting forces from the outside that were disrupting their peace, purposefully or not. Although this was a point of great concern to Cara, she hung in there, calm and supportive, and strangely proud to find that her feelings for Jude were obviously strong enough to face adversity without running.

"I never did get," she said, "why jealous exes always think that horrible behavior and creepy stalking are going to lure a lover back in. If I wanted someone back, I'd be charming and considerate. I'd leave roses at their doorstep instead of dead rabbits."

Jude stared at her, wide-eyed. "Dead *rabbits*?" She pointed to the front door, her face full of disgust. "Please don't tell me..."

Cara shook her head. "Of course not. I was just thinking of that old movie where someone finds a pot on the stove that turns out to contain the boiled remains of their pet rabbit."

"I thought it might be a reference to my work," Jude said. "To Bunny. You know, killing my protagonist as a symbol of destroying my career?"

"You're seeing ghosts," Cara said. "You can't honestly believe she'd travel 9,000 kilometers with a dead rabbit in her carry-on."

Jude shrugged. "I don't know what to expect anymore."

"What does she want anyway?"

"To make me suffer." Jude slumped down on a chair. "It doesn't matter how."

Cara shook her head. "Women can be very vindictive when they don't get their way. Maybe I should have a talk with her."

"Yes," Jude said, "if we want this to get completely out of hand, then we should send *you* to California to set her straight."

"I meant, on the phone," Cara said.

"She was never like this when we were together." Jude shook her head, then she looked at Cara and sighed. "Would you mind terribly if we took a rain check on dinner? I'm really not in the mood for a date."

"Of course I mind," Cara said. "Come on, go change. Put on your dancing shoes. There's no better way to forget about all this than to go out and have some fun." She walked to Jude's chair, grabbed hold of her hands and tried to pull her up. It was like trying to pull up a dead person. "Come on, sweetheart," she pleaded. "It's our anniversary." She kissed Jude's hand. "I've got a whole thing planned."

Jude freed one hand from Cara's grasp and stroked her cheek, a gesture that was condescending more than anything else. "It's not really an anniversary, is it, Cara? I mean, two months, that's nothing really special."

Cara shook her head. "You know what? I would have *made* it special."

꩜ ꩜ ꩜

They didn't see each other all week—Jude was 'tied up.' She canceled again the Saturday after, having an unscheduled meeting with her lawyer in the afternoon and wanting to use the evening to write.

"I thought you had writer's block?" an annoyed Cara said over the phone.

"Which is exactly why I have to sit down at my desk as soon as I feel even the slightest urge to work."

"It's like…literary constipation." Cara giggled.

"I guess," Jude said. "But anyway, I hope you understand."

As it turned out, Cara didn't. She got the horrible feeling that Jude couldn't get rid of her fast enough.

"Maybe we can work on it together," she suggested. "I want to help. I could come over later. Bring some dinner."

"No, honey, I'm sorry. It's not just the writing either. Zoe's been having nightmares and she calls me to her room every three minutes to check for monsters under the bed. It wouldn't be any fun for you."

"There's no law that says I have to have fun all the time," Cara said. "It's not like I'm seven years old and need to be constantly entertained and indulged. I simply want to be there for you. For both of you," she added hesitantly, not sure her presence wouldn't make Zoe's nightmares worse than they already were.

Jude didn't speak, which Cara knew to be a silent rejection of her plan.

"Whatever happened to facing things together?" she said, as a last attempt to get through to Jude. "I am, after all, *the one.*"

She knew it was a bad moment to bring that up, a childish attempt to claim something that had to be earned from day to day rather than be a permanent position that required no effort to maintain. She needed to know if Jude's words had meant anything at all, or if it had just been some stupid, sentimental line that people use in the heat of the moment and then forget about. She broke out in a sweat when she realized that she was, once again, going through the nightmare of seeing a woman morph into the opposite of everything she had seemed to be. Her mind went back to that day in the park. She had marveled at finding someone who was not only gorgeous, but more laid-back than any woman she'd ever been with. She wanted to scream with frustration. How would she find that easygoing person now, under all these layers of misery and doubt and anxiety?

"I'm under a lot of pressure here, Cara."

"So let me help you. Don't shut me out. Let me come over and support you."

"I'm sorry, but that would be counterproductive right now."

Heat washed over Cara—a rush of anger and disappointment, and something more alarming, a feeling as if the floor beneath her crumbled and her life went into a free fall.

"*Counterproductive*? Jude! What the fuck kind of word is that! What am I to you? A business associate who messes up your timetable?"

Jude's sigh was audible. "This is not *about* you, Cara. This is my livelihood. My reason for living. I need to take this seriously."

Cara flinched. She knew very well what Jude's career meant to her, and she totally respected that, but was it really her reason for living? The anger subsided, and the adrenalin seeped out of her, leaving her feeling like a deflated balloon. Her muscles seemed to go limp—she almost dropped the phone. At least it was clear to her now where she stood in the pecking order. Not, apparently, where she deserved to be. Not where she had so presumptuously assumed she already was.

"Very well then," she said. "Good luck, Jude. I hope it will all work out for you."

꒰ ꒱

"I can't believe you dumped Jude Donovan." Myra was so outraged she spilled her tea all over Inge's couch. She lifted a buttock and wiped over the leather with the back of her hand before her angry gaze settled on Cara again. "I thought we went over this? What part of 'don't screw this up' didn't you get?"

"It was good while it lasted, and now it's over," Cara said. "Shit happens. Also, I did not dump her. It was a mutual decision. We're just not in the same place. We want different things at this point in our lives."

Cara tried to sound breezy, indifferent almost, hoping they would all shut up. It wasn't so much the conversation itself that was unsettling—after all, she was used to being grilled about her choices. What made it far more difficult this time was that the breakup had left her sad and cranky. She was feeling hopeless, with the strong desire to stay home, draw the curtains, and drink herself into a stupor. The fact that she had initiated the break up herself didn't change the fact that it was Jude who was responsible for it. Jude had become unavailable and uncommunicative—a stranger. She had shut Cara out, and if she knew Cara at all, she must have known that being shut out was the one thing she couldn't possibly accept or live with.

"I agree with Myra," Alice said. "You know I don't like to interfere in other people's lives, but this woman has it all—beauty, fame, money, and who knows, maybe she'll Bunny her way to a villa with eighteen bedrooms one day." She snorted. "And if you're not in that place, Cara, and if you don't have any ambition to *get* there, then frankly, I'm beginning to doubt your sanity."

Myra moaned. "And to think that Tijmen and Sofie were about to have Jude freaking Donovan sit on the edge of their beds and read them a *Bunny* story that nobody in the world had heard yet."

Cara frowned. "Is this about my happiness or about you guys getting invited to Jude's book launch parties and being offered free holiday accommodation?"

"I'm just saying," Alice said, "that she has everything to make your life perfect."

"You're forgetting that she has a few things to make my life hell too."

"Like what?"

"Like a cranky kid, an insanely jealous ex-wife, and not enough time for me, to name but a few." She took a sharp intake of breath. "But I don't really understand what the big deal is. You know I don't stick around to see real life creep up on the romance! You've always known that. Why should this time be any different?

"Because of who she is," Alice said.

Cara shook her head. "Again, that's all on the outside. And if that's your argument, you're shallower than I thought. She's human like the rest of us. I don't want the image that I have of her now tainted by seeing her in granny panties, fighting a migraine, having a bad hair day, or swinging a hatchet at her poor computer. What we had was beautiful. Too beautiful to watch it go down the drain. I'm done. I've crossed sleeping with a celebrity off my bucket list, and now, if you don't mind, I'm going to get on with my life."

ᕤ ᕦ ᕥ

"A car wash? Please tell me you're kidding."

Cara shook her head. "Magic Auto Clean."

"Your career choices seem to be getting more and more juvenile," said Alice. "What's next? A paper route?"

"We can't all dedicate our lives to things as important as next year's color trends, you know?" She wanted to slap Alice. "Some of us actually have to work for a living."

"Some of us refuse to grow up," Alice said.

"I think it's a fear of death," said Myra, looking at everybody but Cara. "She's always telling us that we're trying to forget about our inevitable demise, but I think *she* is. She figures she can keep it at bay by pretending life will always be the way it was when she was seventeen." She looked smug, as if she were the only one who understood her little sister. "Come to think of it, Cara has always had a little trouble acting her age."

"Hello!" Cara said. "I'm right here! Please don't talk about me in the third person."

"Personally, I believe her subconscious is telling her that she's not good enough for Jude," Alice said, ignoring Cara. "There's a feeling of inadequacy at the root of it all. Which is why she dumped Jude before Jude had a chance to dump her. This way, she doesn't have to think about not measuring up. Which would be too painful for her."

They were sitting outside a coffee house, sipping their lattes. Inge was slumped in her chair, sad but brave. Her voluptuous body clad in loose fit harem pants and a batik print shirt, she was all dangling bracelets and big, frizzy hair. Myra, in another pair of comfortable shoes and another pair of stained maternity pants, was as distracted as always, staring off into space, clutching her ever expanding belly for dear life. Alice was simply her arrogant, bored, short-skirted self, balancing a ridiculously large pair of Ray-Bans on her nose and sipping her coffee with her pinky in the air.

Cara stared at the people passing by their table and suddenly, out of the blue, she realized that her sisters, Alice included, were nothing but caricatures. They had adopted a role, a way of looking at the world, a way of talking down to her that freed them from the burden of having to think about their own lives. They were stuck, all three of them. And she would get stuck with them, always be the victim of their need to control her, if she didn't make some long overdue changes to her life, right now. *They* were the ones having a problem, not her. They were all jealous of her, of her courage to remain free spirited, of her sense of adventure, of her refusal to live her life by anybody's rules but her own.

"You know what?" she said, sitting up. "I'm sick and tired of always getting the third degree from you guys. If I *do* have a fear of inadequacy, it's because you three are constantly shoving my inadequacy in my face!" People were beginning to look at them, but she didn't care. She took a sharp intake of breath. "For the record, I live my life my way, and if you have a problem with that, and if you think it's okay to vent your frustrations about your own failed lives by criticizing mine, then bite me! Go find someone else to kick around."

They stared at her, mouths open.

"And while we're at it," she said, feeling her face getting blotchy with pent-up anger, "I might as well tell you that

I'm seeing Kelly again." She gave them a second to process this information, but she didn't wait long enough to let them speak. "That's right," she said, "*she* was the one who almost got me kicked out of my apartment. Turned out that it was all a misunderstanding. I ran into her, we talked, and now we're seeing each other. And yes, we're having fun, if you guys even remember the meaning of that word. Deal with it!"

She jumped up, knocking over her chair, and trotted off.

Cara spent a lonely night in her apartment, pacing the floor in sheer frustration and not answering her phone, until the incessant beeping and ringing got on her nerves so badly that she picked it up and hurled it across the room. It went skidding down the hall and crashed against the bedroom door. She wasn't going to talk to either of her horrible sisters. *Or* Alice. They were so respectful, so careful, when it came to judging each other's choices, so why were hers constantly scrutinized and blatantly rejected, as if her life wasn't her own, but some kind of shared hobby? Why wasn't Alice the subject of their scorn? Wasn't it far more logical to pass moral judgment on someone who'd been involved with a married man for more than a year, than on someone who was admittedly good at screwing things up, but who at least screwed with her *own* things instead of someone else's? Shouldn't they all take a good, hard look at themselves first? Were any of them perfect enough to have earned the right to throw the first stone? Look at them! One was miserably obese and barren, one was hopelessly superficial and terrified of growing older, and the other one was so afraid of silence that she filled every corner of her home with screeching little brats. And they thought *they* were in a position to tell *her* what to do with her life!

She was doing the right thing. As the hours went by, she was able to convince herself over and over again that she was doing the right thing.

She'd been observing Jude's life from close up, and while she was very sure of her love, she knew that they were bound to fail each other bitterly if she didn't put a stop to things right now. Because the thought that she too would have to adopt the same life, made her choke.

Cara knew that if they continued on this road, she would end up juggling the same responsibilities Jude did. She pictured herself taking care of Jude's manipulative little shrew while Jude was on tour. She imagined Jude and herself as a couple, arguing over whose turn it was to load the dishwasher, struggling to make their mortgage payments, slowly losing interest in each other. Cara had a vision of herself as an administrative assistant in a pantsuit, spending her days on the top floor of one of the impressive, glass office buildings uptown, wondering if a fall from the fifteenth floor would guarantee a quick death. And then there were the angry ex, the Bunny deadlines, and the scumbag currently suing Jude—all the insecurities and the pressure that came with her career. Jude may have been telling the truth when she said she wanted to be both free *and* in a committed relationship, but what did that mean when each day of the life you shared together was nothing but a drab repetition of the one before? Cara knew, that it was only a matter of time before Jude, organized as she was, as she had to be, insisted they synchronize their datebooks, no doubt appalled to find that Cara didn't even own a datebook. Jude would get her one that would fill up with boring obligations: taking the kid to the dentist and the car to the shop, cooking wholesome meals, visiting the in-laws, going to bed at nine p.m., filing tax returns together. They might even be audited. Weren't writers being audited like *all* the time? Would she have to get rid of her shoebox full of unopened bank statements and get used to filing every bill and ticket she ever got in the appropriate binder, categorized by subject? Would she have to enter every penny of the household budget she spent in a spreadsheet? She didn't even know how to work a fucking spreadsheet! They would have stopped talking and stopped loving long before then, and what else was there? Without love, what was the point?

She broke out in a sweat. She began to feel queasy. She thought it might be the flu.

But it wasn't.

ฦ ◡ ꓹ

Jude's voice oozed despair. Cara gritted her teeth and wiped her eyes. She forced herself to listen to the messages over and over again, torturing herself by imagining Jude's lovely face, blotchy and tear stained, needing Cara's comfort, her reassurance, her loving arms around her. She stood firm, because she knew, that as heart wrenching as this was, they'd both be better off in the end if she stood her ground now. It was an act of love more than anything else.

It went on for weeks. Jude would call and call, leaving messages in a half-smothered voice, asking for an explanation, begging for another chance, pleading to get together and talk. Until finally, she just cried. And then, all was silent.

Chapter 10

AT THE BEGINNING OF MAY, on a gentle spring day, Myra gave birth to Ede, who had managed, despite living in the cramped womb she'd called home for so long, to balloon up to an impressive eight pounds.

Cara went to the hospital, guilt ridden because she hadn't been in touch with Myra for weeks. She bought two ridiculously large stuffed animals and a heart-shaped balloon in the hospital gift shop. Her heart was heavy—there was no way of knowing if Myra even wanted to see her. She tried not to think about the possibility that she wasn't welcome, that she'd be sent away. She opened the heavy door to Myra's room just a crack in case her sister hurled a bedpan at her. But as she came closer and saw Myra's gentle gaze, she realized that there was nothing to worry about.

Myra was alone, visiting hour was almost over.

"These," Cara said, putting the stuffed animals, one pink, the other blue, on the bed, "are not necessarily meant to be handed out according to any gender biased rules." She tied the balloon to the bedpost and kissed Myra on the cheek. There was an IV drip in her hand. She looked pale and disturbingly fragile.

There was a transparent hospital bassinette next to her bed. Cara bent over and peered inside at her newborn niece, who looked tiny, despite her considerable birth weight. She was pale more than pink, silently recovering from the arduous task of being born. She was dressed in white, the only color in her wardrobe an impossibly small pink hat. She was fast asleep, her tiny fists resting next to her head. Her eyelids quivered, but she didn't wake. Cara didn't know if this child was somehow different than the others, more special, or if maybe she was extra sensitive these days, but she felt a sudden rush of love for the infant wash over her. Something profound had happened here, something to do with the essence of everything—something that she was somehow a part of. Realizing this made her realize, also, how utterly irrelevant her reason for distancing herself from her sisters, the most important people in her life, had been. Because not only was it a sister's prerogative to give unsolicited advice, but as it turned out, they had been right. Breaking up with Jude really was the stupidest thing she'd ever done.

When she sat down by the bed, and Myra stroked her hair, she couldn't stop the tears from welling up. None fell, she made sure of that—not because she was embarrassed to cry in front of her sister, but because she knew that once she allowed them to fall, they would never stop.

"I've turned into a weepy old woman." She smiled through her tears.

"It's alright, you know, everything is fine," Myra said. "I'm so glad you're here."

Cara hung her head. "I've been a crappy sister."

"Or maybe I've been a crappy sister," Myra said. "I've been going over this in my mind time and again. And you definitely had a point. We do tend to give you a hard time. And we should butt out of your life a little more. I know we only have your best interests at heart, but that's not really an excuse."

Cara nodded, not sure how safe it was to talk about this now. "So how about the baby? Is she okay? Are you?" She put her hand on Myra's arm. "You look drained. And what about the drip? Is that routine?"

Myra nodded. "They're keeping us overnight, but there's nothing to worry about." She nudged toward the bassinette. "The baby's fine. And I'm fine too. Hell, we're all fine. I've done this before, you know?"

"But you sure as hell aren't going to do it again, right?"

Not a sound came from the bed, at least not the 'oh God, no' Cara had been expecting.

"Right?" she repeated. "Jesus, Myra, don't tell me you're considering having more."

"Well, yes and no."

"What the—"

"It's Inge."

A cold fist closed itself around Cara's heart. "Inge? What about Inge?"

"She's had another miscarriage."

Cara's heart sank. "Damn," she said softly. The thought that she hadn't been there, that she hadn't even known, made her feel horrible. She had done wrong by all of them.

"It's killing her, Cara," Myra said. "It's going to be the death of her."

Cara nodded, hanging her head.

"And I can't let that happen. Arend and I have been talking about this for a while now, gathering information and consulting people who've been through it. And we're totally on the same page."

"About what?"

"Surrogacy."

Cara's jaw dropped to the floor. "Sur—"

"That's right!" Myra said. "I've decided that I'm going to carry their child. Inge's and Bart's. If they'll let me. If we can make that work. I'm telling them tonight."

꩜ ꬶ ꙅ

It was Bart who opened the door. He seemed surprised to see her, but he didn't say anything. Once she was inside, he took her coat and gave her a bear hug, the same way he always did.

"I'll be in the den," he said, "if you need me." He turned to walk up the stairs.

Inge was sitting on the couch, her feet resting on the coffee table. The dog, Boy, an adorable mutt they'd rescued from the pound, was lying next to her, his head resting in her lap. The television was on, but she wasn't really watching. She was leafing through a magazine, but she wasn't really reading. Cara knew, even from where she was standing, that Inge was determined not to look in her direction, though she was very aware that her sister was standing there. Cara looked around the room, which was as colorful, cozy, and warm as it always was. Inge and Bart had arranged their lives around having no children so meticulously that it was almost unnatural—a desperate attempt to drown out the darkness and the silence by making a lot of noise and splashing color everywhere. They were socially active, throwing casual dinner parties and hosting informal get-togethers almost every weekend. They were constantly planning and taking trips. They spent a huge chunk of money on making their home welcoming and comforting. But for those who knew, what was missing was always more prominent than what was there. There was simply nothing that would compensate for, or make one forget about, the void in the lives of this couple.

Cara stood there, watching her sister lying under her padded quilt, trapped in a cloud of sorrow. Her heart swelled with a feeling of compassion so strong, it made her gasp for air. And as she recalled Myra's words, the thought that there might just be *one* last chance to see a bouncer seat in this room, a playpen, a floor littered with toys, made her realize that there was nothing in this world that she wanted more than for Inge to have her baby.

She cleared her throat. "Hi," she said, hoping for an invitation to come closer.

It didn't come.

"Hi," said Inge.

"I heard what happened." Cara took a few careful steps. "Myra told me."

Inge turned to her, hugging the quilt closer around her. She was looking old and hopelessly forlorn.

"Oh, honey." Cara practically ran toward Inge. "I'm so sorry."

Inge pushed the dog out of the way, threw back the quilt, and got up, meeting Cara halfway. She practically threw herself into Cara's arms. "I know you are," she sobbed. They stood like that for a while and then sat down, close together, holding hands.

Inge turned her tear-stained face toward her. "We had such high hopes this time, Cara." She shrugged. "What kind of failed woman am I, if I can't even do the very thing that women were put on this earth for—to have babies?"

Cara cleared her throat and stopped herself, with some difficulty, from protesting against the depiction of all members of her gender as glorified incubators.

She took her hand out of Inge's, resting it on her knee instead. "Now listen," she said. "Don't go there. This is simply a medical problem. It has nothing to do with you as a person. Or as a woman."

"I know." Inge hung her head. It was clear that countless people before Cara had told her the same thing. "It's just that…I'm a mother, Cara. I *am* a mother. I just don't have the child to prove it."

Cara didn't know what to say to something quite so sickeningly sad. She sank her teeth into her lower lip until she tasted blood to stop herself from crying.

"But this was it, you know?" Inge sniffled. "This was our last try. Bart is insisting, for my sake, that this is where we give up. And I think he's right." She shook her head, slowly, as if she had a lingering hope of being persuaded otherwise. "No more."

"So now what?" Cara realized that Myra hadn't talked her plan over with Bart and Inge yet.

"There's a new road ahead of us. The road to acceptance. And we're going to meet that challenge head on, Bart and I. We're going to leave it behind us. The hope, I mean. And I'm actually looking forward to that. No hope, no disappointments. Peace."

"Have you…talked to Myra lately?"

"Of course," Inge said. "She left the hospital with the baby yesterday. In fact, I was supposed to see her this afternoon. She said she wanted to talk to me about something. To us, but Bart's leaving in an hour, and he'll be tied up at work the rest of the day." She eyed Cara. "Why don't you and I go together?"

"What if she wants to talk about something private?"

"So? I don't keep any secrets from you."

"Honey...uh...did you happen to notice that we had a big fight and haven't talked in weeks?"

Inge nodded. "Sure. So what? We're family. We fight. And then we make up. It's no biggie, right?"

"Uh...right," said Cara.

Inge brought her face closer to Cara's, studying her. "So how've you been? You look a little pale, but it suits you." She sighed. "It actually makes you even more attractive, in a Scarlett Johansson sort of way. Where are your glasses?"

"I left them at home," Cara said. "I got sick and tired of seeing everything so clearly."

Inge nodded. "Tell me about it." She sank down into the cushions. "But anyway, how's the Jude situation?"

"It's...uh, the same, actually. Over and done."

"And Kelly?"

Cara shook her head. "Not my brightest hour."

"It wasn't the first time around either, honey," Inge said gently. "I figured the second wouldn't be all that different." She seemed to come back to life a little now that she had steered the attention away from her own problems and onto someone else's. This was charted territory to her—telling other people what to do.

Cara nodded. "Still, it was something I seemed to need to get out of my system. It's made me realize and accept that my Kelly days are behind me. I'm too old to get drunk in some sad, dimly lit gay bar anymore, making out with a twenty-two-year-old girl behind a dumpster after closing time; all the while trying to forget that her mascara's run from crying, because someone named Ashley has just told her that she's getting back together with her boyfriend." She sighed. "Too old and too lazy. Or maybe tired is the better word."

Inge pulled a face that might express anything from loathing to admiration—Cara couldn't tell.

"Did you *ever* do that?"

"Sure." Cara smirked. "Didn't you?"

Inge shook her head. "You're odd, Cara. You're a drifter. This is how I see it…" her hand drew a wide circle in the air, "…life is a veritable smorgasbord of tasty experiences, one more delicious than the next. It's a whole spread for us all to enjoy, and *you* refuse to try the metaphorical shrimp."

Cara frowned. "What the hell is the metaphorical shrimp?"

Inge pointed a finger at her. "You think about what that is, okay."

Cara tried, but nothing came to mind. "I'm sorry," she said, "but I've never really been that good at getting your food metaphors."

"The thing is…" Inge sighed, "…you love Jude. You may not want to hear this, but you do. I've always known that. I could tell."

"Oh, really? And how, oh great one, could you tell that?"

"The sheer…I don't know…excitement in your voice when you talked about her. Like you'd found a treasure. Or even better, a passion. A destination." She rested a hand on Cara's arm. "I know you think you can live your life without all that nonsense, honey. I know that we're all on our way to our graves and that girls just wanna have fun, yada, yada, yada…but the truth is, that no matter how cynical you are about the human condition, you have to understand that none of us can live without a sense of purpose. We need to bring meaning to our lives. And she was helping you do that, Cara. She changed you. She made you a happier, more fulfilled person."

Cara didn't speak. Or move.

"Oh, and she made you giddy. But I guess that was the sex."

"Sex hasn't made me giddy in ten years," she lied.

"All I'm saying is that you're not a naturally giddy person."

Cara shook her head. "You got me there."

The dog whimpered in his basket. "It's okay, Boy," Inge said soothingly. "No one's going to harm you, and no one's going to steal your food. Not on my watch."

The dog sighed contentedly, as if that was all the reassurance he needed, and went to sleep.

"Want to talk about your commitment issues now?" Inge shoved Cara teasingly. "While I make tea?" She checked her watch. "Or shall we have wine? I might as well reap the benefits of being barren."

Cara flinched, but she didn't say anything, being among the few people who could certainly appreciate both cynicism and drinking as a way to deal with hardship.

"I thought we were going to see Myra?"

Inge shrugged. "There's time."

"Then can I have a Coke?"

"You sure can, ma'am."

When Inge came back with the drinks, Cara had settled comfortably in the recliner that was her usual spot. "I decided no," she said, taking the glass from Inge. "I don't want to talk about my commitment issues now. Or ever."

"Why not?"

"Because, and I say this in the most loving way possible, you guys tend to think in absolutes."

"Huh?"

"To you, people are either commitment phobic, for whatever reason, or they're not. But it's not that simple. I, for instance, am more than able to commit to someone. What about my relationship with you and Myra? I see you guys like a hundred times a week." She smiled. "When we're not fighting."

"Let's forget about that now, okay?" Inge said.

Cara nodded. "We're always there for each other, day and night. If that's not commitment, I don't know what is."

"That's different," said Inge. "We're family."

"You also seem to think that I have a problem with monogamy. And I don't. I've never cheated on anybody, or felt the need to. Ever."

"So then…what was it?"

Cara didn't know what to say. She twirled the glass in her hand. It was a good question. Good enough to keep her up at night. It was probably what Alice had suggested; she would have disappointed Jude. She wasn't up to par. She tried to forget the fact that Jude hadn't thought she was up to par either. Not by frowning at her career choices, which would have been annoying but tolerable, but by creating an inner sanctum that she could never ever reach.

"What was it," Inge continued, "that made you run when things got serious with Jude, while it was obvious to everybody that you were completely crazy about her?" She put her feet on the coffee table again. "I'm not judging you. And I'm not above admitting that I might be wrong, or narrow-minded. I'm just curious. You find the person who is arguably the love of your life, and you react by freaking out and dumping her. Is that not...unhealthy behavior?"

"Probably."

"Do you suppose it has something to do with Mom and Dad? With Mom's breakdown after the divorce? I mean, you were fifteen! Kids are pretty susceptible at that age. Maybe what you got from that, even subconsciously, was that people can't be trusted. And that you're better off not giving them the power to hurt you."

Cara shrugged. "I don't know, Doctor Phil. Maybe you're right. But I have always known, no matter how much she victimized herself, that Mom was just as much to blame for the breakup as Dad was. I do think it was harder for me, being the only one still living at home and actually having to watch Dad leave, but kids go through that kind of thing all the time." She shrugged. "I don't think it has anything to do with that. I really don't want to be looking for childhood traumas. I simply like my freedom. Because that's just who I am." It wasn't the truth, or at least not the entire truth, but it was all she could handle right now.

"You're a very loveable person," Inge insisted. "It seems like such a waste."

"Or it's the opposite. Instead of giving my love to just one person, I'm spreading it around."

"Excuse me, but what you've been spreading around is not love. It's a ride on a merry-go-round."

Cara wasn't happy being compared to a carnival attraction, but she let it pass, since she was also strangely relieved that their fight hadn't prompted Inge to be a little more careful with her comments. She did, and would forever, speak her mind. And Cara realized that she wouldn't want it any other way. Especially since she was obviously given the same rights—her own rant and subsequent silence were clearly forgiven and forgotten.

"But you did love Jude, right?" Inge insisted. "You *do* love her."

Cara shrugged. "What do you want me to say? That I spend my nights writing cheesy rhymes about her, where I compare her to a summer's day?"

"That sounds kind of sweet," Inge said, "comparing someone to a summer's day."

"It's from a sonnet," Cara said.

"That you wrote?"

"No, that William Shakespeare wrote, actually."

"And you just called that a cheesy rhyme?"

"If he wrote it today—"

"Never mind that," Inge said impatiently. "My point is, you love her. You do love her, right?"

Cara nodded. "I do." She produced a wry smile. "I do indeed."

Inge gulped down her Coke and then shook her head. "You know what your problem is, baby Sis?" she said. "You're an idiot."

Chapter 11

Life went on. That, after all, is what it does best.

Cara was more than ready to move on in the old, familiar way, wanting to leave behind her the feeling of childish excitement at simply being alive that Jude had given her. She had finally landed back on earth, and she had understood the true origin of her bliss—a simple surplus of oxytocin.

But she soon became aware that something had shifted on a level, or in a way, that she couldn't quite control or write down to hormones. The familiar patterns seemed to have lost their pull. Instead of giving her freedom, the way they always had, they now felt restricting, like a wrong-sized piece of clothing she was tugging and pulling at to try and make it fit. She tried to steer herself back on the old track, convinced that the detour she had obviously taken didn't necessarily mean she had to change destinations, too. She was reluctant to surrender to any new way, assuming that what she felt was temporary.

But it wasn't.

Too much had happened. Maybe it was the birth of Ede, and of her strange connection to the child, or maybe it was the arduous project that her sisters were to embark upon. Maybe it was her own reconciliation to them. Maybe it was the memory of Jude, and the pain of losing her. Or maybe it was simply a question of age—of shedding the skin that no longer fit and replacing it with a new one.

Whatever the reason, Cara took a deep breath and started applying herself to being an adult—not so much a different, but a slightly more responsible person, who was willing to embrace, albeit hesitantly, the complexities of life rather than run away from them. There was a mundane level to her transformation too. She opened her bank statements and stored them in a binder. She opened a savings account. She bought throw pillows. And she bought houseplants that she watered with military precision. She researched all she could find on surrogacy, wanting to know exactly what her sisters were up against in the long road to making Inge a mother and Bart a father.

She stopped dating, ignoring the cloaked invitations to one-night stands from the women in her little black book, failing to understand their sudden lack of appeal, and mourning it, but eventually accepting, for now, that casual sex was off the table.

Before she knew it, something she could only describe as a pleasant stability that she refused to acknowledge at first, but that she eventually embraced, was starting to color her days. It earned her a new sense of self-respect.

At night, after a day's work at the carwash, she began to scour the Internet for information on teaching. Her old dream from college mysteriously resurfaced, as she thought about ways to have a grown-up job that she could be passionate about. The longer she thought about it, the more appealing it seemed. She knew there were drab sides to the teaching profession, but the thought that bestowing a love of literature in young people's minds could be her core business was strangely exhilarating.

"Good for you, honey," Myra said, on one of the many visits Cara paid the Koopman household to see baby Ede. "You're going to be great at that. And I know just the place for your internship." Myra was routinely feeding her youngest daughter, the formula bottle loosely in hand, tipping it slightly as it became emptier, adjusting it to the child's needs without even looking.

"What do you mean, an internship?" Cara said. "I need an internship? I know I need a teaching certificate, but I'm a college graduate, so that shouldn't be too hard."

"No matter how you do it, practice in dealing with young people is of the essence, if not required," Myra said. "And I *have* young people. So come babysit next week, okay? I'm taking Arend out for his birthday. I've got tickets to the Ajax game, and I'm going to make dinner reservations at some place that serves those horrible, ten-pound steaks." She stuck out her tongue. "I don't know what it is with men and meat." She put the bottle on the table and draped Ede up over her shoulder, gently patting her back." It's not exactly my idea of a stylish celebration, but this is his party, after all." She smiled. "And he deserves it, my guy. Because he's great."

Cara frowned. "How is babysitting four infants going to prepare me for a teaching position?"

"Young minds are eager minds." Myra rolled her eyes as Ede burped and then spit up on her shoulder. "Rookie mistake," she said. "Forgot the bib." She picked up the baby, holding it in her arms, and turned her head, looking at her shoulder in disgust.

"Hold her, will you?" She gently lowered the baby into Cara's arms and walked out of the room.

"Hi there." Cara placed her niece comfortably in her arms. "Aren't you a little stinker?"

Ede eyed her curiously before a big smile lit up her entire face. "You're Aunt Cara's little, itty-bitty, tiny stinker, aren't you?" Cara went on talking and smiling at the child until she began to giggle, but then Ede lost interest. Cara held a teething toy in front of her face that Ede grasped and put in her mouth immediately.

Cara looked around the room, cradling the little girl in her arms. Myra's house was similar in style and size to Inge's, but even though six people were living here, four of whom were under the age of seven, it was dramatically less cluttered than Inge's. Inge liked that homey, lived-in look. She would fill up every bit of available space with trinkets and knickknacks: souvenirs, scented candles, framed pictures, rugs and pillows, and hand-picked flowers in tiny vases. Whereas Myra not only ran her household with rigid discipline, but showed a strong dislike of every item that would gather dust without being of any practical use. Even her family room was spotless; the walls a gentle beige; the carpet a sensible, stain-resistant orange; the furniture expensive, but practical. She would allow toys on the floor, but only as long as the children were playing with them. As soon as they were outside, at school, or had gone to bed; the rooms were cleared, the toys neatly gathered in toy chests and boxes that were kept behind the doors of a huge, white-washed cabinet dominating the family room.

The door opened. Myra came back with a clean shirt on and her hair in a ponytail. It seemed that she had reapplied her makeup. Subtle though it was, it transformed her face. The slightly shabby look she tended to allow herself when pregnant, always disappeared right after the baby was born. Sometimes as soon as the next day, she turned back into her old, preppy self.

She undid the top button of her blouse. "So do we have a deal? About the babysitting?"

"You make it kind of hard to say no," Cara said. "And I'll do it, as long as it's clear that it's a favor *I'm* doing *you*, and not the other way around."

"Right." Myra sat down next to her. "I can see how I may have been a tad transparent there. Although, I do maintain that being around children of any age is good practice for people in the teaching profession." She smiled at her baby daughter, who seemed very content lying in the crook of Cara's arm, happily playing with her toy.

"So what brought this on?" Cara said. "You've never asked me to babysit before. In all honesty, I thought you didn't quite trust me." She moved her fingers across Ede's tiny hand. The child grabbed hold of Cara's thumb with her free hand and held it tightly. "And I was fine with that," she said. "Taking care of four children without any experience seems like quite a challenge. Frankly, I wouldn't know where to start."

"It's not that I didn't trust you," Myra said. "I just never thought babysitting would be your thing. Now that you come over so often, I see that you're great with kids, no matter how much you deny it."

"Ede's the only kid I'm great with." Cara stroked the child's cheek. "She's my soulmate."

Myra shook her head. "You can't be good with just one kid. You either have it in you, or you don't. And I say you're a natural."

"I wasn't great with Jude's kid," Cara said morosely.

"You never gave that a chance. How many times did you even meet her? Three? Four? You're not supposed to run the first time they show you their cranky, bitchy side. You know? They can be pretty fickle at that age. One day they spit you out, the next, they adore you. They don't have to be civil, like grown-ups. They need to be disciplined and taught in an age appropriate way, how to behave. That doesn't happen overnight, and that's okay. Cut them some slack. They have eighteen years to get the hang of it."

Cara nodded. She wasn't about to tell Myra that she'd ran the very *first* time she'd met Zoe. In fact, she didn't want to discuss the subject at all, even though she'd brought it up herself.

"It's not rocket science anyway." Myra shook her head. "There won't be much to do. We'll make sure they're in bed before we leave. All you need to do is to keep an eye on things. And an ear. We have baby monitors for that. And you may be requested to read the twins a bedtime story."

Cara nodded. "That, I can do."

"You're a life saver," Myra said. "I know that turning forty-two is not really a big deal, and Arend doesn't care about his birthday, but you have to be careful about these things. It's not always easy to find even a moment to be together. In fact, it's downright impossible, but I'm simply making the time. I want us to be more than just parents. It's so easy to slip into that sweatpants rut where you both stop making an effort."

Cara nodded. "I understand," she said. "Do I ever. You guys have a great time and don't worry about a thing."

"You do realize," Myra said, taking back the baby, who was starting to whimper, "that reading the twins a story…" Her voice trailed off as she pushed a pacifier in her daughter's mouth.

"What?" Cara said.

"Will mean reading them a *Bunny* story."

"Uh-huh."

"Is that…a problem?"

"Jesus, Myra! I'm not going to have a nervous breakdown every time I see a *Bunny* book."

"Well, I don't know, do I?" Myra rolled her eyes. "You never talk about her. I don't know if you're completely over her or if you spend your days sitting in a darkened room, pining for her."

"I'm completely over her."

"I know you're lying, Cara. Why don't you give her a freaking call?" Myra shook her head. "For God's sake. You're so horribly pigheaded." She took one of her daughter's tiny feet in her hand. "It's so simple, you know. This is why I can't bring myself to let it rest, because it's so very simple, and you two fools just don't see it. Believe me when I say that no couple is a match made in heaven. I know it sounds horribly unromantic, and it is, but relationships require work. Maintenance. They're like living organisms—they wither if not properly tended to. Everybody over the age of sixteen should know that. You and Jude, without wanting to, have done everything wrong. You both pushed the very buttons that made the other person run like hell. *You*, my dear, are not so much afraid of commitment, as of not being a part of that commitment. You can't handle living by rules and structures that are carved in stone. Which is why you need someone who's willing to *communicate* with you and to make changes when things don't work. And what does Jude do? At the first sign of trouble, the first time her kid has the runs, the first time her ex sends her an angry e-mail, she shuts you out and stops talking. Ergo, you run." She shrugged. "Jude, in turn, is afraid to become dependent on someone's support, because every time she was dependent on someone's support in the past, she didn't get it and crashed to the ground. Don't ask me how I know." She frowned when she saw the inquisitive look on Cara's face. "I just do. And because this is Jude's experience, she needs to convince herself that she can deal with any crisis without your help. You, wanting to show her you're there for her, keep shoving that help in her face. Ergo, she runs." She sighed and smiled, obviously content with her analysis.

"But I—"

"No, I'm not done. This is not hard to solve, you know? Just sit down like two grown-ups and talk about this. Tell Jude that she really can count on you, and ask her, in turn, to keep the lines of communication open at all times and to never shut you out. You'll fall into the same trap a couple of times, fix it, and then, bam—you ride off into the sunset together."

"I—"

"This is simply your response to past…boo-boos, for lack of a better word. Negative experiences cause behavioral patterns that are meant to protect you, but that end up holding you back and that ultimately prevent you from reaching your potential." She patted Cara on the knee. "Classic case."

"Are you done?" Cara scoffed. "Exactly how is it that every single person I know seems to have gotten a degree in psychology overnight? And for the record, I am not pigheaded." She took a deep breath. She was feeling uncomfortable talking about this. She was becoming tired of the opinions and analyses people kept shoving in her face, but it was also a relief to share her grief with someone who seemed to understand it and who showed some compassion.

"The thing is," she said, "I *did* call her. I left a thousand messages on her machine. I texted her. I e-mailed her. I sent her postcards. There was no response."

"Oh, honey," Myra said. She cocked her head in that way that conveys pity. "I had no idea. Why don't you tell me these things? You're obviously suffering. Let me suffer with you. Let's find a way for you to get her back."

"I'm afraid that ship has sailed." Cara shook her head. "At first, when she tried to get in touch with me, I ignored her. I actually thought I was doing us both a favor. But, as the weeks went by, I realized how bizarrely I had overreacted. You were right, it seemed as though she shut me out, but when I think about it now, I realize that maybe I should have simply given her a little time and space." She hung her head. "I'm afraid I've hurt her deeply. I wanted to show her how devoted I was, but what I really did was to show her that I can't be trusted. Anyway, once I realized what a horrible mistake I'd made, I tried to get in touch with her, hoping to talk and reconcile. But it was too late. Jude had chosen to ignore *me*. There's no way she'll talk to me. And who can blame her?"

"Jesus," Myra said. "You know where she lives, right? Why not just go down there and confront her?"

Cara shook her head. "Because it's obvious that she doesn't want anything to do with me anymore. And I need to respect that. I don't want her to think I'm stalking her. It'll only make things worse, especially given her history with Laurie. If I want to make her shut me out of her life forever, then showing up on her doorstep unannounced is exactly what I should do. "

Myra shook her head. "What a mess."

"I have tried to move on," Cara said, "to learn from it, but everything seems so glum now. It feels like every day I wake up, it's Monday morning. And it's always raining."

Myra leaned in and hugged her, careful not to crush the baby. "Poor thing," she said.

They were silent, as Ede made her presence known by making a gentle razzing sound, spitting out the pacifier in the process. Myra picked it up and put it back into her daughter's mouth.

"So, your new…ways," said Myra, "if that's the word— the teaching, the way you're supporting Inge, your new interest in our kids, and that you're not seeing anybody, is that…you know, for *her* benefit? Is it a way to get her back? To show her what you're really made of?"

Cara shook her head. "I haven't morphed into a completely different person or anything. It's just that I've been feeling that the old ways don't seem to work for me anymore. So, I'm making some changes. And somehow…" she looked at the child in Myra's arms, who was sucking on the pacifier which such force that it bobbed up and down in her mouth, "…I sort of fell in love with your daughter."

Myra smiled at the child in her arms.

"But none of these things have anything to do with Jude."

"Of course they do," Myra said. "I always said she had a profound effect on you. She taught you what's important in life."

Cara shrugged. She didn't have the energy to contradict her sister, no matter how wrong she was.

"She's Jude Donovan, Cara," Myra said, stroking her daughter's chubby arm.

"Yes, and I'm Cara Jong. What's your point?"

"Call me a romantic old fool, but I've always had such a good feeling about you two. And I still do, you know. I really think you shouldn't give up so easily. There simply has to be a way to—"

"Forget it, okay?" Cara said. "There's no way. Period."

☽ ☾ ☽

"So these are the baby monitors." Myra pointed to two appliances sitting on the coffee table that looked like tiny robots. "You don't have to run upstairs at the first whimper." She sighed. "That's what we did after we first had Jeroen, but now that we're veterans, we ignore everything but actual deafening screams, smoke alarms going off, or the sound of breaking glass."

"I get it," Cara said.

"You don't have to worry about Jeroen, by the way. He's staying at Arend's parents for the night."

"Does that mean a pay cut for me?"

Myra laughed. "You can help yourself to anything in the fridge." She raised her finger like a school teacher. "As long as it's food or non-alcoholic beverages."

"I'm a grown-up, remember? I have my own fridge, with my own food and my own beverages. Very few of which are non-alcoholic, thank God."

Myra shook her head. "You will have iced tea, or diet Coke."

144

"Are you trying to tell me that once you have kids you can never have a drink again?"

"*We* can," Myra said. "But you can't." She sat down, having failed to manage putting on her shoes while standing on one foot.

"Now listen, Cara, you can't have boys over."

Cara nodded. "Understood. What about girls?"

"Uh…will you be good? Play board games? Do charades?"

"How about strip charades?"

"That's a grey area, but no."

"How about strip Twister? I hear good things about that."

"Ugh," said Myra. "You really should think twice about doing that."

"I'm beginning to get why this job is paying so well," Cara said under her breath. "It's like having a tiny prison sentence." She saw Myra eye her critically.

"I'm joking! You're being ridiculously nervous about this. I've been babysitting since I was practically a baby myself."

"And then you went on a fifteen-year sabbatical," Myra said. She picked up her keys from the coffee table and hollered upstairs, "Arend! We're late!" They heard him stumble around above their heads. "I swear that man needs more time to get ready for a date than I do. He's every bit as dainty as his sister. If he doesn't come down looking and smelling fucking gorgeous, I'm going to be really pissed."

It took them another half hour to actually leave the house. It was strangely quiet after they left. Cara couldn't recall being alone in Myra's house ever before. She went upstairs to check on the twins and to read them the promised story. As she walked past the nursery, she lightly brushed the door with the back of her hand.

The twins began to holler the second she opened the door to their room. Cara put a finger to her lips. "Shush," she said. "The baby's asleep."

"Shush," the twins said. It didn't sink in right away, but somewhere in the back of her mind, Cara registered that something about the pattern on the twins' pajamas was very familiar. As soon as she came closer, she realized what it was. They were *Bunny* pajamas. She hadn't known that such a thing existed. Bunny's image was bouncing all over the place—small Bunny's, large ones, upside down ones, Bunny eating a carrot, riding a bicycle, playing in a sandbox. The pajama feet were actually two tiny white rabbits. It was adorable, but, Cara admitted to herself, confusingly painful at the same time. She shook it off—life was much simpler if you didn't allow yourself to make a drama out of every little thing.

She couldn't make out if Myra had dressed her niece and nephew in these particular pajamas on purpose, to send some kind of subtle message, or if it was simply a coincidence; but she came to the conclusion that it was probably the latter, because as she walked around the room, she stumbled upon other merchandise—a sippy cup, a bib, two pairs of fuzzy slippers.

Both kids were sitting up in bed, anything but drowsy, excited at the prospect of manipulating their rookie babysitter aunt into letting them stay up past their curfew.

"Bubby," Sofie said, pointing to the bookshelf above the two cribs that ran the length of the entire wall. She shrugged her small shoulders. "Daddy shoe."

Cara looked at the collection and selected the infamous *Bunny Has a Boo-Boo*. She positioned her chair exactly between the two cribs.

"Boo," Tijmen said. He got up and swung his leg over the side of the crib, where it got stuck. It wouldn't be long, Cara realized, before he'd figure out how to climb to his freedom.

"Let's not do that, okay?" She picked him up and put him back. He didn't start crying, as she suspected he might. He accepted his fate like a man.

Cara opened the book and began to read the story she knew so well.

After a couple of pages, the twins grew restless and started to make silly noises to draw each other's attention. They were both standing in their cribs by now, their little hands on the railing, until Tijmen let go, landing flat on his padded behind. He began to collect his stuffed animals in his arms and started throwing them on the floor one by one.

"Do you guys know," Cara said, turning over the book and pointing to Jude's picture, "who this is?"

Both children stared at the picture, Tijmen with his mouth open.

"Mommy!" Sofie yelled.

"Nooo," Cara said. "This is not Mommy. It's Jude."

"Doooo," said Tijmen. He blew a big bubble.

"Jude is actually the writer of this book, did you know that?"

Both children stared at her dumbfounded.

"You didn't, huh? Well, she is. She's also the writer of *all* the other Bunny books."

"Bubby," Sofie said.

"Right, Bubby. She's the writer of *Bunny Finds a Friend,* too." Cara leaned over to the kids, who seemed to suddenly concentrate on her words. "You know what's a funny coincidence? After Jude wrote *Bunny Finds a Friend,* she

147

found a friend of her own. Is that an unusual story or what? They *do* say that life is stranger than fiction."

"Yay," Tijmen said, putting his arms in the air.

Cara followed his example. "Yay," she said. "That was certainly worth a cheer. Because that friend, you see, was me."

Sofie nodded.

"You're probably wondering," she said, looking at the little girl, "what happened?"

"No," Sofie said. She shook her head.

"I'll tell you anyway," Cara said. "I fucked it up again. Just like I knew I would."

"Fuck," Tijmen said.

"Oops, strike that." Cara stared at him, shocked. "I did not just say that, sweetie. Let's not use the f-word here. Let's just say I couldn't make it work, okay?"

"Duck home," Tijmen said.

"And now she's gone."

Sofie held up her hands, palms up, as if she meant to say, 'what can you do.'

"And the truth is, I want her back more than anything. All I want is a chance to make up for what I did wrong, but I don't know how to do that. She won't even talk to me."

"Bubby," Tijmen said. "Bubby poo-poo."

"Let's focus here, okay?" Cara said. "There has to be a way to find her again, to at least sit down and talk. Don't you think? She's not just anybody, you see? She's smart and funny and lovely. And gorgeous too!" She held Jude's picture in front of Tijmen's face again. "See? Isn't she beautiful?"

Tijmen grabbed hold of the book and threw it on the floor. Cara bent over and picked it up. "So," she said, "any ideas?"

Tijmen let out a scream. "Bubby poo-poo!" It was obvious that his patience was running out.

"Okay," Cara said as she opened the book again. "you're absolutely right. I guess we should get on with it. Thanks for listening, you guys. That really helped. So let's see what we can do about Bunny's boo-boo, if not mine."

Sofie clapped her hands as Cara continued reading.

Chapter 12

CARA DIDN'T KNOW WHAT TO think when she was summoned to be at Inge's place on a Saturday at nine in the morning with an overnight bag. And she *really* didn't know what to think when she walked in the door and saw her sisters and Alice standing at the far end of the living room, leaning against the mantle. They were all wearing jeans and hoodies. And boots. Even Alice. They looked like they had just robbed a bank and were arguing about how to divide the loot.

"If this is an intervention," Cara said, eyeing them suspiciously, "I have no idea what for." She took off her coat and hung it in the hall closet. "Honestly. I'm an upstanding citizen. I have a respectable job. I keep a sensible diet. I'm *celibate*, for God's sake—I'm as close to death as I could possibly be."

"This is not an intervention," Myra said, walking up to her. "It's a surprise."

"Really?"

"Uh-huh," said Alice. "We're going on a little road trip."

"A road trip? Where?"

"That's for us to know and for you to find out."

And then they shrieked like seventeen-year-olds on spring break.

꩜ ☋ ꩜

"I don't get why we're going on a road trip in a decrepit Volvo when one of us has a brand new Mercedes sitting idly in the driveway." Cara nudged Alice, who eyed her wearily. They were stuffing their luggage in the trunk of Inge's car, struggling to get it all in.

"We're not snooty enough." Inge rested her entire weight on her suitcase. Cara watched her as she locked eyes with Bart, who was observing them from behind the window of their kitchen. Inge blew him a kiss before she went back to cramming the luggage in the trunk. Cara smiled. It seemed that they were even closer now that the road to surrogacy had recently culminated in the transfer of two embryos—two embryos that Cara imagined floating in some no man's land between life and death inside Myra's body. Cara's admiration for Myra was boundless now that she knew all she had been willing to go through to make Inge and Bart parents. And what she was willing to go through still. There were no guarantees, though. At this point, all they could do was wait.

"And besides," Inge said, "I'm sure I'd spill tartar sauce on Alice's velvet seat covers if we took the Mercedes. I'll feel a lot more comfortable driving my old clunker. My seat covers are used to being soiled and thrown up on."

"Ugh," said Alice. "Please, tell me you're joking. Please, tell me I'm not going to spend more than three hours sitting on some random person's old puke."

Inge shrugged. "Would you rather be sitting on fresh puke? Because that can be arranged, you know."

"More than three hours?" asked Cara. "Where the hell arc you taking me? I didn't bring my passport—maybe we should swing by my place and get it?"

"No need," Myra said. "The travel time includes rest stops. And it's no secret. We're driving all the way south to our beautiful province of Limburg." She opened the car door and climbed onto the back seat, resting her enormous purse in her lap.

Cara sat down beside her. "Limburg, huh? As much as I love forests and streams and hills...why?"

"Their traditional pies," Myra said. "Sweet flan."

"Really? We're going all this way to eat pie? A whole weekend?"

"What can I say? I have a craving."

Cara shook her head. "You don't even like pie."

"Oh, for God's sake." Myra closed the car door. "Let's just go, okay? Before I change my mind."

Alice sat down on the passenger seat, and Inge took her place behind the wheel.

"So where in Limburg are we going?' Cara asked. She was suspicious—there was something mysterious about this trip, something they weren't telling her.

"Maastricht," Inge said. "And Kerkrade."

"Why Maastricht and Kerkrade?"

"Because." Inge looked at the printout of her route.

"Because what?"

"Because our hotel is in Maastricht and our *thing* is in Kerkrade."

Cara didn't know why, but her heart began to pound. "What thing is that? Are you having me committed?"

Inge shook her head. "There's an abbey there. Very old and very beautiful. We thought we'd take a tour." She looked up from her paper. "And no, we're not having you committed. We're going to have fun. Our hotel is situated near an idyllic, cobblestoned square with a fountain and old-fashioned street lamps and lots of bars and restaurants. Also, there's an indoor ski center practically around the corner."

"That's great," Cara said. "But I've never skied in my life and I have no intention of starting now." Also, she had never had any particular interest in old abbeys. Not enough to drive more than 200 kilometers to see one, anyway. There was definitely something fishy going on.

"Is there something you guys are not telling me?"

Myra sighed. "Cara, honey, could you just sit back and enjoy the ride? Could you do that for me?"

Inge started the engine.

"Are we taking the A2?" Alice asked as she fastened her seatbelt.

"No." Inge shook her head. "The A2."

"Didn't I just say—"

"I know what you said!" Inge adjusted her seat. "I was trying to make a point."

"What point?"

"That I'm driving, and that what I say goes. I'm not discussing my chosen route with any of you."

As Inge drove off, Alice took the printout from the dashboard and studied it. "I can't believe you're not using normal, twenty-first-century navigation." She flapped the piece of paper in front of Inge's face.

"Not discussing it," Inge sang.

Alice put the printout back on the dashboard. "Your route isn't the fastest one, you *do* know that?"

"Today is not about speed, it's about spending quality time together." It was clear that there was no room for suggestions—Inge was at the helm and that was the end of it.

"This is going to be fun," Alice said under her breath.

"It is." Inge ignored the sarcasm. "We'll make a few quaint stops along the way, don't you worry."

"Quaint stops where?" Cara said.

"Honey, I could explain it to you," Inge said, "but since you have the sense of direction of a firecracker, I suggest you just enjoy the ride and leave everything to me, okay?"

"That sounds delightful," Myra said. "But please, make sure there are plenty of gas stations along the way for me to use the restrooms at."

"Oh yummy," said Alice. "Germ filled, gas station restrooms."

"No problem," Inge said, driving off. "There will be lots of breaks. We have all the time in the world."

"Maybe you should add a couple of hours to those three." Alice leaned to the left and looked for Cara's face in the rearview mirror. "We might not even get there before nightfall." She took a tissue from her bag and tried to wipe the window clean. "Wouldn't hurt to see a little something on the way."

"I love it when we bicker." Cara nestled comfortably in her seat. "It's just like old times. Just the four of us, going on an adventure. I'm going to forget that there's something you're not telling me. Spending a weekend away with you guys is exactly what I need. What we all need."

"That's what this trip is all about," said Inge. "We are, after all, the four musketeers. Musketeer...rettes." She raised a fist in the air. "Divided we stand, united we fall."

"Isn't it the other way around?" Alice asked. "United—"

"Jesus," Myra said. "Can we just get on with it? I feel queasy already, and we haven't even left the city yet."

◖ ◡ ◗

Traffic was light and there wasn't much to see—miles of ivy-clad noise barriers, billboards, distribution centers, grassland with grazing cows and sheep, a car crashed into the safety barriers with a police car behind it, a shoe in the emergency lane, a clear sky with puffy clouds. It was an uneventful, hazy, autumn day. Even so, Cara felt that there was something in the air. A promise. A glimpse of a future that was alive with light and joy. She couldn't explain it, it was just a feeling.

Inge insisted they play guessing games and sing, but when nobody joined in, she turned on the radio. She scanned the frequencies until she found a station that played hits from the eighties and nineties. It wasn't long before the music took them back and they started reminiscing, their thoughts drifting off to days long gone—high school, family life, crushes, sibling rivalry. Their hair. And their clothes. They laughed, both embarrassed and amused, as they remembered Cara's cargo pants, Myra's chinos and ballet flats, Inge's Champion sweatshirts. The tight ponytails and the large hoop earrings.

"I wish I could have known you guys back then," Alice said.

"Remember your grunge phase?" Myra eyed Cara lovingly.

"I'm surprised you even know I *had* a grunge phase," Cara said. "You can't have said more than four words to me during your senior year at high school." She scoffed. "And if I remember correctly, those four words were 'don't touch my stuff.'"

"I'm sorry." Myra put a hand on Cara's knee. "I was just so busy back then. You have no idea."

"Busy sneaking out of the house every night in your ultrashort miniskirts." Cara smiled. "I know. I used to see you scurry across the grass when I looked out my bedroom window. I never told Mom and Dad, and you never thanked me."

"I had that thing with Koen back then," Myra said. "And I don't think Mom and Dad would have cared one way or the other. They were too busy fighting to notice us."

"Was it really that bad?" Alice asked.

Myra nodded. "Why do you think I got married so young?"

"Because you were crazy in love with my brother?' Alice suggested.

Myra grinned. "That too."

"But first there was…Koen?"

"Yes," Cara said, "and Jan, and Tim, and Martijn, and Ivan, and—"

"Hey!" Myra shook her head. "Don't make me out to be some kind of—"

"What?" Cara said innocently. "These are just the ones I know about."

"I believe in playing the field a little before settling down," Myra said. She looked at Cara critically. "And I think you're hardly the person to be throwing stones. Anyway, before Arend came along, I was convinced that Koen was the love of my life." She smiled dreamily. "He played hockey, he was politically active, and he had this really aristocratic hair."

Inge snorted. "Aristocratic *hair*?"

"Yeah. You know, Hubbell Gardner hair. Hubbell was—"

"Yes, we know," Alice said. "The guy in your favorite movie from 1814. And yes, we know it's a timeless classic."

Cara sighed. She didn't know why.

Then Myra sighed too. "I wonder what's become of him."

"Maybe he has a Facebook page," Inge said.

"Nah," Myra shook her head. "I'm not going down that I-wonder-if-ex-has-a-Facebook-page road. I'm happily married, and I intend to keep it that way."

"Who else did we have who was the love of your life?" Cara asked. "Who was the guy with the soul patch who used to bring Mom flowers when he picked you up?"

"Oh, God, yes, Evert!" Myra clapped her hands in excitement. "Evert with the soul patch and the cigarillos. He was dead set on becoming a poet but his father insisted he take over the family business. It was right out of a romance novel." She stared in the distance, a dreamy expression on her face. "He drove a Honda CR-V. *Great* car." She cleared her throat. "Interesting fact—did you guys know that I lost my…uh…you know? To Evert? In that car? He had the most amazing blue eyes. Like pools of clear water."

"Really?" Inge half turned her head, momentarily taking her eyes off the road. "Evert? In a car? How very raunchy. And unbecoming."

"It was different for you," Myra said. "You got engaged at age three! You weren't open to adventure the way we were."

"I've always been happy to find my soulmate so early in life," Inge said. "But anyway, all these years, I thought Kasper was the proud recipient of your flower."

Myra looked disgusted. "Kasper? Honestly? Kasper, the king of BO?"

"Is it my turn to say ugh yet?" Cara asked. "Can I crack open a window?" She stared at the overpass ahead.

"What about you then, honey?" Myra turned to Cara. "Who did you unravel the mysteries of Sapphic bliss with?"

She produced a roll of Lifesavers from the pocket of her coat and offered Cara one. "And how exactly does that work?"

Cara almost choked on the piece of candy. "How it works?" she said, once she'd stopped coughing. She stared at Myra. "Do you want me to get…technical?"

"Please do," Inge said. "For instance—"

"Please don't!" Alice yelled.

Inge pushed Alice's knee out of the way, opened the glove compartment and took out a piece of chocolate, wrapped in silver foil. She held it up. "Anybody?"

"No!" they yelled. Inge removed the wrapper, keeping just her elbow on the steering wheel, and put the whole piece in her mouth. She let the wrapper drop to the floor.

"Would it be too much trouble to keep your hands on the wheel and your eyes on the road here?" Alice dug her nails into her thighs. "I don't know about anyone else, but personally I do not have a death wish."

"I'm an experienced driver," Inge said. "I could actually do this with my eyes closed and my hands behind my back."

"What a surprise it would be to our loved ones if we all came home in body bags," Alice said.

Cara considered that if Alice came home in a body bag, her boyfriend would at least still have his wife to console him. And somehow, for the first time since she'd known about this, her heart went out to Alice for the hopelessness of her situation, regardless of any moral indignation anyone might feel.

Myra shook her head. "What I actually meant to ask," she said, turning back to Cara, "is how you…met girls. How you hooked up. How did you recognize each other? Who asked whom on dates? I don't mean now that you're out and

158

you've been around the block a couple of hundred times, but back then, when you were in that process of finding out how things work. Hell, you were new at this too, once. I never saw you as anything but a baby back then, and by the time you were old enough to start dating, I was long since married."

"She was very secretive," Inge said. "Even after she came out, I never actually saw her with anybody."

"I went through my rites of passage just fine without you guys," Cara said.

"Was it like in that movie?" Inge munched on the chocolate. She checked the outside mirror and changed lanes.

Cara shrugged. "What movie?"

"That movie that we saw about the two college girls who nurse a wounded bird back to health in some foggy, enchanted forest?" Cara saw Inge's eyes rest on her in the rearview mirror. "I remember that it ended horribly, but I forget how."

"They both got married to balding, overweight investment bankers," Myra said.

Inge shook her head. "I think one of them killed herself."

"Oh, come on, of course it wasn't like the movie," said Cara. "Nothing as dramatic as all that." She sighed, like she always did, when confronted with straight people's tiresome ignorance. It wasn't so much that they were ignorant, but that they were both arrogantly and condescendingly so— using their indisputable right as the superior breed to ask stupid questions as often as they liked under the pretense of being open-minded.

"People always think that relationships between girls are either tragic and doomed, or all about sex," she said. "While usually they're neither. It's just two girls getting together, no different from a girl and a guy getting together. They study, they argue, they do laundry, they even get colds. If you didn't know any better, you might mistake them for regular people."

"There's no need to get snappy," Myra said. "So who was it?"

"Who was what?"

"Well, you must have dated when you were old enough. So who was your first? I mean your first…interest?"

Cara paused for effect before she answered. "Remember Claire?"

"Claire…Claire…" Myra shook her head, then she punched Cara. "Not that sissy who lived down the street from us? What was her name? Welders? Belders? The one with the angelic face and the pink, frilly dresses? The Barbie?"

Cara smiled. "I can see why she might have slipped under your gaydar, but somewhere between her frilly dresses phase and her own grunge phase, we became really good friends. *Really* good friends."

"Inge!" Myra hollered. "Did you hear that? Cara did a little parallel parking with Claire Welders!"

"Oh please." Cara stuck out her tongue. "Do you have to call it that? Aren't we a little old to resort to—"

"Claire Welders?" Inge yelled, keeping her eyes on the road as requested. "Goody-Two-shoes herself? Wow. That makes me so proud!"

"Stop screaming, okay!" Alice pressed a hand against her ear. "Do you want me to arrive in Limburg with a ruptured ear drum?"

"So how did you…?" Myra moved a little closer, touching Cara's arm with her own.

"Well," Cara whispered, "she invited me to her house one night—"

"For a playdate," Inge hollered.

"She needed someone to help her prepare for a math test. Her parents were out for the night. She was wearing something that could easily be misconstrued as a negligée, and she was burning so many candles I was afraid I'd walked into a séance."

"And then what?" Myra sounded breathless.

"Well, after it became clear to both of us that we shared a hobby or two, we made out."

"You made out, huh?" Myra took a moment to let the information sink in. "So did you know how to do that?"

Cara laughed out loud. "How to do that? Actually, yes. Not to blow my own horn, but I've always been pretty good at that."

"I thought that maybe, when you're young, and you don't really know what to expect from a woman—"

"That's probaly one of the perks of being gay," Inge interrupted. "You already know where everything is." She giggled. "And how it works."

Cara shook her head. "It's not easy to keep the mystery alive around you guys, is it?"

"Wow," Myra said. "Claire Welders was stunning."

"I don't know if you've noticed," Alice said. "but Cara's pretty stunning herself."

Myra shrugged. "I guess you're blind to that sort of thing when it comes to your own sister." She cast a glance at Cara. "But now that you mention it," she said, with barely concealed admiration, "she *is* kind of stunning." She put her hand on Cara's arm. "No wonder you landed a gorgeous and famous American writer."

"Yes, well…" Cara squirmed in her carseat. "Could we… talk about something else? Please?" She was trying hard not to think about Jude as it was. The last thing she needed was someone reminding her. She wasn't sure why Myra did. Was she afraid she'd forget Jude? Did she think that such a thing was possible? She shook her head. She didn't want this. She wanted to focus on the weekend, on having fun in Limburg with her sisters instead. And why wouldn't she? Surely she was leading a fulfilling life where the absence of romantic love wasn't necessarily a problem? She had goals now. She had plans. The future was stretching out before her like a vast ocean of endless possibilities.

But as the radio started playing "Lady in Red," they all fell silent, and she couldn't help but think about Jude.

The trip down memory lane seemed to have made all of them pensive. They drove, for miles and miles, in a bubble of silence, each woman immersed in her own thoughts.

They made three stops at gas stations within the next two hours. Cara got out of the car to stretch her legs. Alice walked around talking on the phone; Cara presumed the calls were to her boyfriend. There was no way of knowing for sure, since she stayed well out of earshot. Every time she hung up, and Cara asked her if she was okay, she blinked in that tired way of people who are actually not okay, but don't want to talk about it.

Inge used the breaks to fill up the tank and buy candy. Myra, who kept insisting that she was feeling sick to her stomach and 'generally weird,' used every break to visit the bathroom.

When they got hungry, Inge exited the freeway and drove to downtown Den Bosch, where they had an early lunch and did a little shopping. At Cara's request, they wandered into a very large bookstore. It was an old building, three stories high, with creaking wooden floors and cast iron, spiral staircases. It reminded Cara of Mrs. Beldam's store, which had been like a miniature version of this one. She remembered how exciting that day had been, with all those unexpected wonderful things happening—meeting Jude, having Jude look at her with pride in her eyes, and amusement, and something that may have been love, even then. She struggled to keep her thoughts from going back to the way that night ended, knowing full well that it wouldn't do her any good to relive those moments now.

She scrabbled for the feeling she'd had earlier, back in the car, the feeling of hope and contentment, but she couldn't find it. She shook her head, forced herself into the here and now, and looked for the nearest distraction. Books!

She was leafing through an anthology of lesbian erotica, when Myra walked up to her from the children's section with a book in her hand. Cara didn't know why, for she wasn't a particularly shy person, but as she saw her sister approach, she quickly put the anthology back. She picked up a random book from the table she was leaning against—a biography of Hillary Clinton, as it turned out.

"Did you know that Jude Donovan has a new book out?" Myra was frowning. She seemed almost indignant that she hadn't been informed of this personally.

Cara swallowed hard. So Jude had obviously conquered her writer's block. She realized that she'd been half hoping, half fearing, that Jude would never be able to put a word to paper again after their breakup. Now that she saw the brightly colored book with the bouncing white rabbit on the cover, her heart swelled with pride at the thought that Jude had come through regardless of everything that was holding her back. She had conquered her demons—she had, as Cara had so unceremoniously told her to do, 'simply sat down and done the job.'

"No," she said, trying to sound indifferent. "I don't generally read the Bunny Chronicles."

This was true. She had learned the hard way that opening Jude's website at least once a day, reading her blog, staring at her picture, remembering all the things they had done, imagining all the things they hadn't done but that she wished they had, didn't exactly help her move on. Which is why she had gone cold turkey. Which is why she had missed the publication of a new book. Now that she was staring at it, she couldn't stop a sudden flood of memories from washing over her. She saw Jude's face with a hundred different expressions on it, one slowly merging into another—smiles morphing into frowns, joy into anger, tears into bliss—and she saw her own face next to Jude's, as if she was watching a kaleidoscopic image of all their moments together. One memory was singled out—the day they had argued about Cara's alleged lack of respect for children's literature. She remembered trying to help Jude overcome that strange and sudden loathing of what had been her passion for so long. Jude had shared with Cara her fear of running dry, of the creativity her livelihood depended on suddenly disappearing to never return. She'd stopped talking and had started to touch Cara, the subject making her edgy and fearful. Their lovemaking, colored with a tinge of sadness, had enabled them to reach a new level of intimacy. Cara remembered feeling almost guilty for relishing the state that Jude was in—there was something languid and hyper sensual in the way she was touched, and although Cara knew it was brought on by Jude's desperate attempt to immerse herself in something that would chase away her demons, or at least keep them at bay, she had basked in it nevertheless.

"Hey!" Myra brought her face so close that Cara could almost count the freckles on her nose. She pointed at the rabbit on the book cover. "I said, funny you should say that!"

Cara shook her head to chase away the disturbing images. "Why?"

"Because this book is a Bunny volume, but it has the glummest title ever." Myra held the book in front of Cara's face.

"'*Bunny Cries*,'" Cara read.

"See? Now what kind of depressing title is that? For a children's book! And did you see who it's dedicated to?" Myra opened the book and read, "*To my muse, wherever she may be.*"

Cara stared at her sister, wishing she would go away, wishing everybody would go away, so she could crash to the floor and just stay there, until she died. Somehow, she kept standing. She even managed to maintain her composure. "That's weird," she said, her voice trembling slightly.

"Very weird," Myra said. "Do you suppose it's a hidden message?"

"I—"

"Oh, my God." Myra looked at her wide-eyed. "What if it's a hidden message to you?"

"Nah," Cara said, shaking her head. "She's just being dramatic."

Myra shrugged. "You're probably right." She tapped the nail of her index finger on the book in Cara's hand. "I wouldn't recommend this, by the way. It's a little garish."

Chapter 13

"HERE WE ARE." INGE MADE a sharp turn and drove into the parking lot of the hotel, where she planted her Volvo in the first available spot.

It was late afternoon. The sun was low on the horizon and there was that typical smell of autumn in the air—the deep and herbal scent of earth and mushrooms and rotting leaves and wood burning fireplaces. Cara stuck her head out the window and inhaled deeply. She loved this time of year. And she loved being away. She'd been in dire need of a change of scenery without realizing it. As usual, in any new situation, her thoughts drifted off to Jude—a strange and slightly alarming habit, given the circumstances. It was almost as if she were observing life through Jude's eyes, as well as through her own.

She wasn't sure if Jude had ever been to the south, to Limburg, which was so uniquely different from the rest of the country. She imagined spending a romantic weekend together, taking long walks through the hills and valleys, following trails along murmuring brooks with water mills and age-old farmsteads. Trying the local delicacies at rustic inns. Spending the night together in an enchanting B and B.

After indulging the fantasy for a second, she fought to push the images away, because she knew from experience that daydreams would turn into nightmares at the realization that Jude was gone from her life. Only this time, it was even harder than usual to stop herself from reminiscing. Having seen the new Bunny book made the memories come to life and it made them shine, as though they'd been dusted off and polished. It had made her realize that Jude wasn't a person from her past at all, and that she should stop trying to convince herself that she was. Maybe it was better to accept and acknowledge the pain—at least it was honest. At least that way, she could stop kidding herself. She might as well admit that the thought of spending the rest of her life without Jude made her feel as desperate as ever. It was pretty obvious that *she* was the muse the new book was dedicated to, and she wasn't sure if this made matters better or worse, but she decided on worse. To pine for someone was one thing, but to know that that person was pining for you just as badly, while there was no way to connect with them, was so much more than just painful—it was, somehow, a cosmic unfairness.

"Hey! Cara!" Myra pushed her. "Are you with us?"

"Totally and completely," Cara said.

Inge snapped open her seatbelt and opened the car door. "This, ladies, is the end of our trip." She smirked. "Please, don't forget to tip the driver." She put her nose in the air and sniffed, like a wolf detecting the scent of its prey. "Ah," she said, getting out of the car, "autumn. Don't you just love it?"

"Is there a drugstore here somewhere?" Myra struggled with her seatbelt. "I need to find a drugstore."

"Run out of tampons?" Inge inquired.

"Oh yuk, do we have to talk about this?" Alice shook her head. "Can't we all just take care of our sanitary needs in private?"

"Stop whining, okay?" said Myra. "You prude. It's not tampons I need. Thank God."

"What *do* you need?" Cara said.

"It's private."

"Do I have it? Could I lend it to you?"

Myra broke out in a fit of laughter. "I doubt that very much," she said. "Besides, it's not something one tends to borrow."

"Are you...in a great hurry getting it?"

Myra shook her head. "Tomorrow will be fine. There's no rush."

They all got out of the car and looked around, taking in their new surroundings. The hotel was a large, modern, glass and chrome monstrosity, at least ten stories high. Nobody said anything as they stood staring at the brightly lit entrance.

"What?" Inge said.

Nobody answered.

"Oh, come on, you guys! This was a spur-of-the-moment kind of thing. I hardly had the time to find some quaint B and B in a castle on a hill, with a wishing well and a flock of grazing sheep outside our window!"

"I was actually taking a minute to admire it," Alice said. "I know this chain of hotels well, and they're excellent. Clean, large, efficient, and full of competent staff."

"I like it too," Cara said. "Look at this." She turned around, the others following suit. "We're smack in the middle of town. It's full of restaurants and bars and old-fashioned street lanterns and happy people, just like you promised. What's not to like?"

Inge opened the trunk of the car and they all flocked around her to get to their luggage.

"Great," Alice said, "my whole beauty case has been dented by all your stupid heavy bags. Why pile everything on top of something so delicate?" She stroked the thing as if she was afraid it might be in pain.

"You're going on forty, sweetheart," Myra said. "Your beauty itself is about to be dented. Permanently. And please, allow yourself to sag a little." She touched her right breast with the back of her hand." It's so…liberating."

The lobby was a welcoming place with a large front desk and lots of comfortable chairs, and tables with glossy magazines to read. There was a view of a bar on their right. Behind them was a dining hall where a man in chef's whites was setting the tables for dinner.

The elderly woman at the front desk checked Inge's reservation. "Let's see," she said. "You booked a deluxe, family room for four."

"Four?" Myra said, looking over Inge's shoulder. "We're all bunking together?"

"It's *deluxe*!" Inge gave Myra a slight push with her elbow.

With the practicalities over, they took the elevator to the ninth floor. Their room really was deluxe, with four single but large beds, an impressive wall cupboard to hang clothes, and a spectacularly large bathroom with a hot tub. The window had a view of the city and the hills in the background.

"I may well move here," Cara said. She took some clean clothes for the night from her suitcase and then pushed it under the bed with her foot, deciding not to go through the trouble of unpacking if they were only going to stay the night. Then they all took turns taking a shower, changed, and went down to the lobby to discuss their plans for the evening.

In their absence, the elderly woman at the front desk had been replaced by a stunningly pretty, dark-haired girl in her mid-twenties, who flashed a dazzling smile at them.

"Maybe you should ask her to join us," Myra said, when she saw Cara staring at the girl. "Or at least close your mouth."

Cara blushed and shook her head.

Myra smiled. "She actually looks a little like a young Jude. I guess that's your type then, huh?"

Cara shrugged. "Let it go, okay?"

They decided to have dinner in one of the many restaurants downtown, and to go for drinks afterward.

"We're not going dancing, are we?" Myra said as the doors of the lobby slid open.

Inge shook her head. "No. Why? Did you leave your dancing shoes at home?"

"I don't know." Myra shrugged. "I feel like I left my stomach at home."

They stepped out into the cool night air—a crescent moon lit up the darkening sky.

"It's pretty chilly in this neck of the woods." Alice hugged herself.

As they were crossing the square, Inge reached into her handmade, quilted purse and produced a city map that she flashed in front of Cara's face before she unfolded it. "Did you know that there are some great gay bars here?"

Cara shrugged. "So?"

"We thought it might be nice to take a bit more interest in your...you know, world," said Alice.

Cara caught up with her. "You make it sound as though I'm living on a different planet from everybody else."

"Let's walk, okay?" Myra took the lead. "And argue about this somewhere inside, where it's warm."

"After dinner," Inge said, "we're going for drinks at a place that has live music. She smiled. "Jazz." She slapped her thigh. "Hot, smoky jazz."

"Jazz?" Cara made a face. "That's great, but jazz tends to have a special kind of effect on me. Which means that you guys have to *promise* you won't let me get drunk. Not even a little. If I do, I'll give you more trouble than I'm worth." She looked at Inge. "But anyway, I thought you wanted to go to a gay bar. Is it...gay jazz?"

"It's gay friendly," Inge said. "Or rather..." She checked her notes. "Open-minded."

"Can't get much vaguer than that," Cara said.

Inge nodded. "It's an open-minded bar that happens to have live jazz tonight."

"Does that mean I won't get bashed?"

"Oh, come on," Alice said, "who gets bashed anymore? You people are always so dramatic."

Cara pushed her. "If you really want to take an interest in my world, I suggest you stop referring to us as *you* people.

"Sorry. You people are always so touchy."

"Would you people be terribly sorry," Myra said, who had hardly spoken since they'd left the hotel, "if we went for a light dinner? Just thinking about food makes me want to hurl, actually."

"There's a permanent TMI alert on this trip," said Alice.

"Light?" There was a bit of panic in Inge's voice. "Light as in...a club salad and a club soda?"

"Is there no gay friendly...like Chinese food place?" Myra looked doubtful. "1 might manage a little kung pao chicken, or something."

Inge consulted the city map again. "There's an Indian place nearby." She kept her finger at a spot on the map. She peered into the distance, then pointed north. "It's that way." She turned, the others followed. "It's a shopping area, you may well find a drugstore there, too."

"How is Chinese the same as Indian?" Cara muttered under her breath, following them.

The first thing they saw when they rounded the corner was a drugstore with an *Open* sign in the window.

"Wait here." Myra practically ran toward it. "I'll be right back." She came out looking very content. She had obviously found what she was looking for.

Once at the Indian restaurant, it turned out to be closed for the season. Because of the cold, and because Myra convinced them that she really needed to sit down, they decided to go to the seafood restaurant that was round the corner from the Indian place.

Cara hesitated by the door.

"What's wrong?" Inge said.

"I wonder if it's wise to eat seafood so far from the sea," she said. "Can it really be fresh?"

"Ever hear of ice?" Inge was trying to push her inside. "And besides, you eat taco's all the time. And Mexico is a hell of a lot farther away than the sea."

"That makes absolutely no sense at all." Cara shook her head.

"You know what, girls?" Myra walked past them and pushed open the door. "Argue all you want, but let me through, okay?" She walked inside and sat down at the first empty table she saw. "It's delightful," she shouted at them.

They all went inside. They were shown to a different table at the back of the restaurant, next to a giant fish tank filled with huge lobsters, claws bound, that seemed to stare at them reproachfully. The sight of them depressed Cara. To appease them, she studied the entire menu for a vegetarian dish, but failed to find one.

"Can I just have a baked potato and a salad?" she asked their waiter. He looked at her as if he was considering asking her to leave the premises, but he wrote her order on his notepad without a comment.

"I'll have the same," Myra said. "Without the baked potato. So basically just a salad. With the dressing on the side."

Inge restored the good spirits of the cranky waiter by ordering the seafood special. Alice had the scallops.

Cara made a quarter turn to the left in her chair so she wouldn't have to see the maltreated lobsters. They gave her the creeps.

"Isn't this cozy?" Myra said, when the drinks were being brought. She raised her club soda in the air. "To us, girls."

They toasted, and then Myra put her glass down, pressed a hand to her mouth, got up and stormed toward the restrooms.

"What's her problem?" Alice asked. "She's been acting weird ever since we got in the car."

"Maybe she's worried about leaving your brother behind with four children," Cara said. "I don't know how the poor man's going to cope on his own."

"Hey," said Inge. "Don't do the crime if you can't do the time."

The food had been served by the time Myra came back from the bathroom. She was looking a little pale, but a faint smile curled at the corners of her mouth.

She sat down without speaking, taking a piece of lettuce from her plate and putting it in her mouth.

"What took you so long?' Inge said. "And what's with all the cloak and dagger?"

"We're a little worried," Cara. "You don't seem quite yourself."

Myra was smiling from ear to ear now. "Nothing's wrong," she said. "I just wanted to be sure. That's why I needed to find a drugstore."

"I don't get it," Alice said.

"I bought a pregnancy test," Myra explained. "And guess what? It's positive."

Inge, whose hand was on its way to her mouth with a shrimp the size of a boomerang, went deadly pale. Her hand went limp and fell on the table; the shrimp was catapulted to the floor.

Myra smiled from ear to ear. "How about that, huh?" She leaned over and kissed an astonished Inge on the cheek. "Congratulations, honey," she whispered. "It seems you're having a baby."

Chapter 14

"CAN WE WALK THERE? To the gay friendly jazz club?" Alice checked her phone for the gazillionth time, as they were waiting for the waiter to bring them their check.

"Bar," Cara corrected. "It's a bar, not a club."

"Whatever. Can we walk there?"

"Can we please, please, please just go home?" Inge wiped the tears from her eyes. "So I can tell Bart? I want to be with him and share this. And not over the phone either. I want us to go shopping for cribs."

"It's early days, honey." Myra put a hand on her sister's arm. "Don't freak out now, okay? You'll give Bart a heart attack when you come home in the middle of the night with your face all puffy. Let's just stick to the plan and do what we came out here to do. On Monday, we'll tell Bart, and you can come with me when I see the doctor."

"What do you mean," Cara said, "do what we came out here to do? What did we come out here to do?"

Inge shoved an obviously startled Myra. "To bond," she said. "To reconnect."

"Again," Alice said, "can we walk to the damned bar or not?"

Inge shook her head. "No," she said, her voice unsteady. "It's too far."

Alice called a cab. It picked them up outside the restaurant in less than ten minutes. The driver was the chatty kind—a proud native, who liked to talk about the region and the town and how all his ancestors had worked themselves to death in the coal mines.

"There go ten minutes of my life I'll never get back," Alice said after they got out of the cab. "I thought he'd never shut up. How much does anybody want to know about how his father, and his father before him, came home looking like they'd fallen asleep in a tar pit? And what's with the accent? I almost had to put my ear to his mouth to understand what he was saying."

"You're not much of a people person, are you?" Cara nudged Alice. "I'm not sure I want to bunk with you when you're this cranky."

"Maybe I'll camp out in the lobby then." She eyed Cara. "Or maybe you should camp out in the lobby. Next to your receptionist girlfriend with the smoldering eyes."

"Stop trying to fix up Cara, okay?" said Myra.

"Sorry," Alice said. "I forgot."

They stood on the curb, staring up at the banner that was hung over the entrance of the bar, announcing the live performance—tonight only—of Maxine After Dark.

"Forgot what?" Cara said.

"Nothing," said Alice, shaking her head. "Never mind. Can we please go inside now, before I freeze my ass off?"

The bar was crowded. The sticky heat after the cold from the street, the smell of liquor and cologne mixed with a tinge of sweat, nearly took Cara's breath away. Myra began to gag before she was even inside. Inge put a possessive hand on her sister's shoulder and another on her stomach. Myra wrestled herself free of Inge's grasp, waving her arms around.

Cara realized how old they had become. And how... weird. How caught up in their lives they were. They would never again walk into a place like this with their minds solely on the evening to come; on getting drunk, on hooking up, on looking smashing. They were women now. She smiled as she realized that this amused her more than it disturbed her. There were plenty of things going on in her life for her to feel good about right now. She had responsibilities and prospects. She had a secure job, where students depended on her. She was supporting her sisters in their joined baby adventure, every step of the way. What it all came down to was that she was a positive factor in the lives of other people, and there was nothing more rewarding than that. She felt as if she finally *was* up to par.

But she also knew what was missing from the list. Though she struggled to push away any memories of Jude, she couldn't help but realize how ironic it was that Jude was gone from her life now that she finally did have something to offer.

The band was playing. It wasn't the promised hot, smoky jazz, but something louder and more upbeat. Cara had no idea what it was—Dixieland? She knew very little about jazz.

They found what was probably the last remaining free table at the far corner of the bar, where they couldn't actually see the band. Not that it mattered. The rousing music was loud enough as it was, and sitting closer to the stage wouldn't exactly be a treat. Cara had been a little worried about her tendency to get sentimental on nights like these. It was a perfect night for great emotions—emotions she knew it would be far better to control.

"Margarita's all around," Alice yelled as soon as they sat down.

"Are you crazy?" Inge said. "We can't drink! We're pregnant!" She put her hand on Myra's stomach. Myra pushed it away.

"There's absolutely no reason why you shouldn't have a drink," Myra said.

Inge shook her head. "Anything you can't do, I won't do."

Alice sighed. "Two hot cocoas it is."

Myra shook her head. "Hot cocoa, ugh, no. Iced tea please."

"So who's with me? Cara, you seem to be the only person here who's not a hundred-year-old or knocked up. Care to join me?" Alice got up and eyed the giant liquor cabinet behind the bar. "They seem to be pretty well stocked here." She turned to Cara. It was obvious that the sight of all those bottles lifted her spirits. "Order anything you like."

"A margarita will be fine," Cara said. "It'll be just like old times."

Alice clutched her tiny handbag firmly in her hand and started pushing through the crowd to get to the bar.

"I'm not sure I'll be able to keep anything down," said Myra. "But I'll give the iced tea a try." She looked pensive. "I never felt like this when I was pregnant with any of my other kids." She smiled at Inge. "Then again, this is not my kid." She half got up from her chair and craned her neck to see the band. "I wasn't exactly expecting this kind of music," she said. "I thought it would be more like a mellow kind of jazz. You know, sex jazz."

"Not sure what sex jazz is," said Inge, "but there will be late night jazz later, with Maxine After Dark. These guys are just the warm up act." She bounced up and down in her chair. "I like it. It's so upbeat."

"You'd find a funeral upbeat right now." Cara looked at her sister's face, and she had a hard time not tearing up when she saw the look of complete bliss.

"I guess I would," Inge said, beaming.

"So what about the alleged gay friendliness of this place?" Cara thought it would be wise to change the subject before they all burst into tears.

"Well…" Inge said. Cara followed her gaze, but the only thing she saw that was even remotely gay were two women who were more or less dancing together—admittedly, dancing like friends, without touching each other. Inge nudged her head in their direction.

"They don't count," Cara said. "Those are two very straight girls hoping to catch the attention of two very straight guys."

"The main thing is that we're all having fun," Myra said. "No matter what our…persuasion."

"Hm," said Cara.

Alice came back with the drinks, frowning. "I wish people would bother using some deodorant before they shoved their smelly armpits in my face, you know?" She put the glasses on the table. "Honestly, is that too much to ask?" She placed the tray on the floor under her chair and sat down. "Anyway, a toast."

"Let's just drink, okay?" said Cara. "We're all getting way too emotional here."

"To life," Myra said. She raised her glass, the others followed.

"Life," they said.

It was one of those moments, Cara mused, when you imagine destiny taking a picture. A snapshot of that very last moment before everything changes.

The Dixieland band played for an hour before the stage was cleared. Cara got up and wandered over there to see what was happening. A new band replaced the old one, bringing with them a whole array of instruments: saxophones, guitars, a trumpet, a clarinet. The piano stayed.

The lights were dimmed. A large woman in a dark-green, glitter dress walked onto the stage. She grabbed the microphone and said a few words that Cara couldn't understand.

It was as if the whole atmosphere changed as soon as she began to sing. All those happily yapping people were quiet the second her slow voice began to waft over the audience. The seductive sound of the saxophone filled the air, and it was as if the night itself was changing clothes—replacing its brightly colored daytime attire with a long, dark, velvet gown. Cara stood staring at the stage, swaying slightly to the rhythm of the deep, lazy voice, and realized that this was exactly what she'd been afraid of. She was too emotional and too lonely to be unaffected by it. She thought it might be a good idea to head back to her table and to suggest leaving for the hotel.

She made a half turn and stood there, her back to the stage, wondering how she would find her way out. She looked to her left, where it seemed she'd have a slightly better chance of escaping. She scanned the faces in the crowd, and as her eyes latched onto something familiar, her heart seemed to stop.

The second Cara saw her, she told herself that she didn't really, couldn't possibly, see her. She knew that the woman she was staring at was a mirage, a figment of her imagination, brought on by her emotional state, by the alcohol, and by the deep desire she was feeling, tonight more than ever, to be with Jude—to talk to her, to touch her, to fall at her feet. Her mind was playing tricks on her—it *had* to be. The woman in the black dress and the denim vest, who stood in front of the stage no more than ten feet away, was *not* Jude Donovan. But it was. It was her, down to the last detail. Even the scar on her temple was visible. She was more familiar to Cara than any sight in the world could have been. The image of her was permanently etched on Cara's brain to the last detail. At the same time, she was a stranger, oddly distant. Cara found it almost impossible to imagine, staring at the swaying figure with the straight, black hair and the piercing, hazel eyes, that they had ever so much as exchanged a word. Let alone shared everything two people can possibly share. She was real. But she was also an apparition.

Cara struggled to keep her breathing under control, as she tried to tear her eyes away from the woman that was Jude, but couldn't be.

"Hey!" A tall man with a glass of beer in his hand eyed her angrily. "You're stomping on my foot."

Cara landed back on earth slowly. She stared at the man's face, finally registering that he was angry, and why, and stepped aside. "Sorry," she said.

She was panicking now. She was choking here, in this heat, with all these people towering over her, infusing her with their sickening smells and sounds. She knew, that if she didn't get some air soon, she was going to faint. She used her elbows to force the crowd apart, pushing people away, pissing them off, receiving a blow to the head with an elbow, and feeling countless shoes stomping on her feet. All the while, the singer's sweetly honeyed voice ridiculed her.

After what seemed like hours, she finally managed to free herself from the crowd that had formed an almost impenetrable half circle in front of the stage. She took a few deep breaths, forcing herself to calm down. When the nausea and the dizziness began to subside, she made her way back to her table, where she practically fell down on her chair. Once seated, she started to panic again. If this was what happened to her when she *thought* she saw Jude in a crowd, than how the hell would she ever get over her?

"What the hell happened to you?" Inge brought her face closer. "You look like you've seen a ghost."

"I have," Cara said. All the color had drained from her face.

"What do you mean, you have?"

"It was…" Cara shook her head. "It was as if I saw Jude. I mean, there was someone in the audience. It was Jude. To me. But it really wasn't, I do know that." She was glad to realize that there was obviously a sliver of sanity left in her.

"Jude?" Alice pulled a face. "Oh my God. Already?"

This wasn't the reaction Cara was expecting. She was expecting her friends to say that it was time she had her head examined. "What—"

Myra put a hand on her arm. "Honey," she said. "I'm sorry. This wasn't supposed to happen. You weren't supposed to see her until tomorrow." She cast an angry look at Inge. "Why the hell did you bring us here anyway? Didn't you know that this was bound to happen?"

"Right!" Inge said. "Blame me! How was I supposed to know she'd be hanging out in a bar in a city she has no business being in. Her conference tomorrow is miles from here. Shouldn't she be in her hotel room getting a good night's sleep?"

Cara wanted to shout at them to shut up. And to *please* tell her what was going on. Even if it was that her mind had finally snapped, or that they were in some bizarre twilight zone for the lovesick. But she had no voice. She opened her mouth, but nothing came out.

"Could you two stop bickering for a sec?" Alice said. "Cara really doesn't look all that well."

"Let me." Myra snatched a tissue from her purse, dipped it into her iced tea, and started rubbing Cara's forehead.

Inge shook her head. "I fail to see how applying iced tea to her face is going to do her any good."

"It's the closest thing to water I have," Myra said. "And it'll do just fine. Being a mother will teach you to be creative too, don't you worry."

After she'd wet Cara's forehead, making it all sticky, she started patting Cara on the cheek. It did the trick. Cara woke up from her reverie and found her voice. She pushed Myra's hand away.

"Stop hitting me!" She took a deep breath and exhaled slowly. "Now will somebody please tell me what the hell is going on here?"

"The woman you saw was probably Jude," Inge said.

"How? What?" Cara shook her head. "You know I believe in coincidence, but even I draw the line *somewhere*. Why are you guys not more surprised to find her here?"

"Because that's why we're here," Alice explained. "We're here, because she's here."

"I...I don't get it." Cara wiped her forehead.

"Let me explain," Myra said.

"Please do," Cara said. "And don't leave out any of the details."

Myra said, "Inge, give me the brochure." Inge handed it to her faster than a nurse hands the scalpel to a surgeon. Myra folded out the colorful leaflet. "Look." She laid it out on the table for Cara to see.

"*Welcome*," read Cara, "*to the ninth annual Dutch Literary Festival.*"

"The festival is popular and draws quite a crowd," Alice said. "It starts tomorrow. It's held in a different town each year and it has a different theme each year. This year's theme—"

"Don't tell me," Cara interrupted. "This year's theme is children's literature."

Myra nodded. "We read in some magazine that she'd be attending, so we thought we'd take a little trip together, have some fun, visit the festival, and hope that you and Jude would bump into each other and that...well..."

"That nature would take its course," Inge added.

It was the first time in Cara's life that she honestly didn't know what to do to her sisters—hug them or bash their heads in.

"I can't do this right now." She got up and trotted off. "Don't!" she said, when she saw from the corner of her eye that Alice and Inge were getting up to follow her. "Don't come after me. I'm just going out for some fresh air. I'll be back soon."

Once in the street, where she could still hear flares of music coming from the bar, her nerves calmed a little. She took a deep breath, the cold air making her gasp.

She had never smoked, but she wished she had a cigarette now. It would be fitting for this particular scene in the weird play they seemed to be acting out.

The door behind her swung open—a gush of heat and sound oozed out, then was muffled as the door closed again. She didn't bother looking behind her, assuming that whoever had come out would pass by her and be on their way. But nobody passed by her. Which is why she turned, expecting to see Inge there, or Alice, or both.

But it wasn't. It wasn't Inge. Or Alice. And there was no mistaking the voice for a stranger's.

"Of all the gin joints..." Jude said softly behind her.

There she was. Jude. She was everything—Cara saw that now. She was water and food, she was rain after a drought, she was comfort after pain—a mirage, a destiny.

She shrugged. "I don't believe in fate."

Jude's gentle gaze found hers. "Perhaps you should."

Cara shook her head. "Fate is actually my loyal, but deluded sisters, orchestrating this."

Jude shivered, reminding Cara of the night they kissed on the bridge. She wished she had the power to erase everything that had happened after that moment—begging the Gods for a chance to start over and get it right this time.

Jude kicked against a cobblestone with the tip of her boot. Her hair fell across her face—she tucked it behind her ears, and although Cara must have seen her do so hundreds of times, the simple gesture brought a rush of desire.

"They orchestrated this?" Jude said. "Didn't you tell them that this thing between us is over and done with?"

This thing. Ouch. Cara cringed.

"I did," she said, "but they're hardheaded. They can't believe that even I was stupid enough to let you go."

"I see. So why did you?"

Cara shrugged. "There are many answers to that question, Jude, but the one that's closest to the truth is that I'm an idiot."

Jude shook her head. "You're not an idiot."

"Oh, but I very much am."

"You freaked," Jude said.

Cara nodded.

"I guess, in a way, so did I."

"So why didn't we tell each other this?"

"Maybe we're both idiots."

"Maybe," Cara said. She paused. "People tell me I'm stuck in unhealthy behavioral patterns." She shrugged. "I don't know, they're probably right."

"Are those the same people who tell you not to shop at Ikea?"

Cara grinned, then she remembered something. "Oh!" she said "I took your advice. I bought throw pillows. And houseplants."

Jude smiled. "Really? And?"

"You were right. They've livened up the place beautifully."

"Great," Jude said. "I would love to see it sometime."

Cara didn't know if she was just being polite, nor could she make out if the conclusion that they were both idiots meant that this was goodbye to Jude. She pegged her for the kind of person who was careful not to repeat previous mistakes. Also, months had gone by. Jude had written a new book, maybe she had moved on in other ways as well. Maybe, all that remained for them to do was to wish each other well. She felt her palms getting sweaty, despite the cold.

"So how have you been?" she said. "You look really well. I've never seen you wearing a dress."

"Few people have." Jude looked her over. "You look well too. You look lovely, actually. I like your hair like that."

"There are times when I try to imagine your face," Cara said, "and I can't."

Jude didn't speak.

"So…" Cara said. The door to the bar opened. Two young men walked out. One of them took a step toward Cara, but before he could open his mouth, his friend grabbed him by the sleeve of his coat and dragged him away. They were both struggling to keep their balance.

"You were saying?" said Jude, when they were out of earshot.

"I…uh…was just wondering…" Cara cleared her throat, "…if you're okay. If you're…you know…happy. If I…can ask you that. I really hope you are. I guess you're seeing someone new by now."

Okay, it was transparent. Cara didn't care. After all, what better time to take risks than when you have nothing left to lose.

Jude shook her head. "No. I'm not. I'm not seeing someone new. Or old. I thought I'd give myself a break from love. Like the rest of my life. How about you?"

Cara looked up at the stars, considering her answer. "Would you believe me if I told you I entered a convent?"

"Really? You know what they say nuns get up to after dark, don't you?"

Cara shook her head. "No. What?"

"Never mind."

"How's Zoe?"

"She's good. Better. Well behaved actually."

"What happened?"

"I guess it was mostly...good parenting." Jude tapped herself on the shoulder. "And lots of bribes." She shrugged. "Or maybe she just snapped out of it. I guess it was a phase. A recurring phase, no doubt."

Cara looked down at the cobblestones, glistening in the moonlight. "I guess so," she said. "Tell me. Do you...hate me?"

The strange question hung awkwardly in the air between them.

"What?" Jude shook her head. "No, of course I don't *hate* you." She stretched out her hand as if to touch Cara's face, but then she reconsidered and pulled back. "I could never hate you," she said.

Cara was almost sure that if this strange encounter led to a friendly goodbye and nothing else, she would want to die on the spot. "If it helps," she said, "I've been miserable the whole time we were apart."

"That actually does help a little."

Cara looked at the cold night sky. Gazing at the stars always made her dizzy. "I can't believe we meet again," she said, "on this magical night. Here. In Limburg, of all places."

Jude smiled. "Instead of on Amsterdam's illuminated make out bridge."

Cara nodded. "You were always funny."

"You too. I've missed that."

"Really? What else have you missed?" Cara said.

Jude hesitated. Cara was afraid she couldn't come up with anything. But Jude actually blushed a little when she said, "Well...the sex comes to mind."

"It does," Cara said. "In fact, almost daily."

"We were so..." Jude took a deep breath, "...compatible, don't you think?"

"We were *mind-blowingly* compatible," Cara agreed. "We owe it to…" She reconsidered. This was not an appropriate joke to make now. She shook her head. "Never mind."

"No, you're absolutely right," Jude said. "We owe it to… etcetera."

They cleared their throats simultaneously, then grinned together.

"You know what else I've missed?" Cara asked.

"What?"

"Your delicious home cooked meals."

Jude threw her head back and laughed. "That is so cruel," she said.

They were silent, shivering in the cold. "I wish," Cara said finally, "that we could have talked. I wish we could have at least given ourselves a chance to do that."

"We're talking now."

Cara nodded.

"So what would you like to say?"

She paused, weighing her chances. "Only that I'd give my right arm for another chance."

Jude frowned. "Exactly what use do you think I might have for a one-armed lover? A left-armed one at that."

The word lover, because it was so out of context, given their caution, sent an unexpected surge of arousal through Cara's body. She shivered.

"Well?"

Cara couldn't believe that Jude managed to keep her tone so light and playful when it might just as well have been spiteful and accusative.

"Actually," Cara said. "I have a little more to offer than that now."

"Really?" Jude said. "Tell me, what did you add to your already dazzling resume?"

"Well, don't freak out, but I've actually become—"

"What? A drug runner? A time traveler?"

"A teacher." She blushed.

Jude's eyes grew wide. "A teacher? How'd that happen?"

"It was just...time, I guess. I applied myself. I teach literature. And I love it."

"That's great," Jude said. "Wow. That seems so... fitting. Do your students know about your addiction to romance novels?"

"That's a well-kept secret, actually." Cara laughed. "And you...wow. You applied yourself, too. You wrote a new Bunny book!"

"The saddest one yet," Jude said. "Have you seen it?"

Cara nodded. "Myra pushed it in my face when we stopped at a bookstore on the way here."

"And?"

"And...is there any chance you'll write a *happy* Bunny book dedicated to me some time? Or is that—"

"I'm not going to write anything ever again if I don't get out of this cold soon." Jude wrapped her coat around her more tightly. Her breath made clouds in the air. "Here's what we'll do," she said. "I'm staying at the abbey."

"So there really is an abbey? I thought my sisters were full of it."

Jude shook her head. "No, there's definitely an abbey. It's both a convention center and a hotel. It's where I'm staying, and where I'll be speaking tomorrow."

"Speaking," Cara said, impressed. "You'll be speaking."

"It's a beautiful place. I was actually wondering if you would join me for a drink there."

"Now?"

"Yes, now."

Cara's heart was doing summersaults. "I would," she said. "Can I have a minute, though?" She pointed to the door of the bar. "My sisters are in there, and I need to tell them I won't be going back to the hotel with them."

"Maybe you should thank them for their…help. I'm not sure we could have done this without them."

Cara nodded. "Yes, I guess their absurd little scheme worked to a fault." She paused. "A lot has happened between me and them actually. That's a story for another time. Why don't I come to your hotel in an hour or so? We're staying at a place downtown."

Jude smiled. "Does that mean you have some sort of curfew?"

"No," Cara said. "I'm free as a bird." She paused. "Does that sound presumptuous?"

Jude shook her head. "Not at all."

"I'm afraid I won't do right by you," Cara said suddenly. She froze, startled by her own words.

"I invited you for a nightcap, sweetheart," Jude said. "I didn't propose marriage. Let's just have a drink, okay? And then we'll take it from there." She slipped Cara a piece of paper. "This is the address of the hotel. The driver will know." Her voice was a little husky. Maybe it was the cold. Then again, maybe it wasn't. "Find me, okay?" she said. "I'll be waiting."

Cara put her hands on the door to the club, ready to push it open.

"Oh, and Cara…"

Cara turned on her heels. Jude took a step toward her, leaned over, and locked her into a loving embrace.

"I've missed you so *very* much," she whispered into her ear.

∩ ◡ ◗

She walked back into the club. It was even hotter than before, and her skin began to tingle. The band was on a break—the stage empty save for the now strangely lifeless instruments.

Cara walked to their table. Her chatty sisters didn't say a word. She didn't sit down. They looked up at her.

"So?" Myra said at last. "Cat got your tongue?"

"We talked," Cara said. She put both hands on her heart. "Thank you *so* much, guys."

"See?' Inge said, "I told you this would work." She leaned over, reaching for Myra's stomach.

"Honey," Myra said, "we really need to establish some boundaries here. I can't spend the next eight months or so having you grope me every time you get excited about something."

"Sorry." Inge grinned, then got serious. "The thing is, that's our daughter in there."

Myra tapped her on the shoulder. "It is, honey. Or your son." She turned to Cara. "So, now what?"

"So, now I'm going to see Jude in her hotel and have a drink with her."

"There goes our roomie," Alice said. "But that's fine. I'm sure we'll manage without you. Just remember your curfew, okay?"

"I have a great idea," said Inge. "Why don't we leave Cara behind in Jude's loving arms and go home. I mean the three of us. It's killing me that I can't tell Bart about the baby."

She lunged for Myra's stomach again, then reconsidered and pulled her hand away.

"It's fine by me," Alice said. "Why stay at the hotel without Cara?"

"Hey!" Inge and Myra protested.

"What!" Alice said. "What fun are you guys? As much as I love you both, all you've done on this trip so far is cry, pee, and throw up. I heard they're giving out a flood warning."

"There's no way we're driving home in the middle of the night," Myra said. "This is my last chance for what may well be eighteen years to stay the night in a hotel without any of my kids. I'm not going to give that up. And besides, I want to go to the convention tomorrow. I think I've more than earned the right to finally shake hands with Jude Donovan."

"She'll be speaking," Cara said proudly.

"See?" Myra said to no one in particular. "She'll be speaking." She winked at Cara. "If somebody doesn't wear her out tonight, that is."

"We're having drinks," Cara said. "Nobody is going to wear anybody out. I'll take a cab back to the hotel later, okay?"

"Really?" Myra said. "Honey, you're going to be sipping wine on a cold night in a romantic, thirteenth-century castle with the love of your life, and you want me to believe you're coming back to the hotel to spend the night with *us*?"

ᕧ ᕤ ᕥ

She gave the driver the slip of paper with the address of the hotel on it.

"The abbey is a popular place tonight," he said. "I seem to be going back and forth a lot. Are you one of the writers?"

"I'm not," Cara said. "I'm just a fan."

"I see," he said, driving off. "Then I hope you get lucky tonight."

Cara looked out into the dark night, and smiled.

"I have a feeling I will."

Chapter 15

Eighteen months later

"I ACTUALLY HAVE GOOSEBUMPS." INGE shivered and held out her arm for Cara to inspect. "See?"

Cara glanced at her sister, who was sitting next to her, briskly rubbing her arms. She had dressed for the evening, wearing a wide, purple sweater dress over black leggings. A multi-colored, beaded headband kept her unruly hair in place. Her eyes were shining with excitement. There was something decidedly festive about her.

Myra, sitting next to Inge on the other side, exhaled loudly. "Goosebumps? It must be a hundred and twenty degrees in here." She frowned. "Or is the hell of menopause upon me already?"

"Not from the cold." Inge turned and looked around. "From the excitement that Jude Donovan is my sister-in-law."

Myra smiled as she glanced at Cara. "I know. She's mine too."

They were sitting in the front row of the auditorium— not because of any VIP status awarded them, but because they'd been the very first ones to arrive. Jude had disappeared somewhere backstage, after numerous break-a-leg wishes from the friends, a hug from Zoe, and a good luck kiss from Cara over which they had all swooned.

They'd been sitting in the front row, just the five of them, surrounded by rows and rows of empty seats that Cara didn't doubt would all be filled within the hour. Cara was, by now, more than used to sitting in the front row of auditoriums, libraries, and bookstores. It always gave her the feeling as if she was somehow protecting Jude. It was ridiculous, she knew, but she was like a buffer sitting there—anyone with wrong intentions would have to go through her first.

She wasn't sure if people recognized her—the occasional picture of the two of them would appear in magazines or on the Internet, but Cara knew very well that people tended to forget who was dangling on a famous person's arm unless that person was somehow of interest, too. And Cara Jong, teacher slash muse slash part-time mother, pretty though she was, wasn't tabloid material. She was happy with her role in the background, although Jude would mention her in every interview she ever gave. She would always refer to her, call her an inspiration, the one person she always leaned on. It took Cara a while to get used to so much praise. She couldn't quite make out which feeling was stronger, pride or embarrassment, but the pride had won. She had even managed to learn how to ignore her sisters when they teased her about how she had turned from a promiscuous woman of the world into this hopelessly boring, suburban housewife.

"We asked you," Inge had said, "to consider bringing a little more stability into your life, not to hook up for all eternity, semi-adopt a child, get a dog, and turn it into the *snoozefest* it is now."

"The dog wasn't planned," Cara had said. "Although we love him to death."

She smiled as she realized how life has a way of throwing things in one's lap. She hadn't been able to stop thinking about the Labrador retriever in Almere, even after she'd called on the neighbor. Knowing that there was room neither in her apartment nor in her life for a dog, she had forced herself to let the matter rest, but since she couldn't get the animal out of her mind, she had decided to try and find out what had happened to him. When she learned that he had been collected by animal welfare and was staying at a shelter, where his future was uncertain, she had picked him up the very same day and taken him home. They'd been inseparable ever since.

Next to her, Zoe was squirming in her chair. Cara had gone over the protocol with her. They had a set of rules for this kind of occasion that they had drawn up together, although she and Jude rarely took her to any event that was too big, or too long, for the child to sit through without getting hopelessly bored or falling asleep. She stroked the girl's hair. "Are you excited?" she said.

"When's Mommy going to come back?" Zoe's bright, blue eyes looked up at her.

"She's not coming back here until later," Cara said. "She's not going to sit with us, she's going to be sitting over there." Cara pointed to the stage, where the sound people were walking around, adjusting microphones, and dragging endlessly long power cords along the wooden floorboards. "See those chairs?" Cara said. "Mommy will be sitting in one of them. Another lady will be sitting in the other one and will talk to her through a microphone."

"What's a microphone?" Zoe asked, but she couldn't be bothered waiting for the answer. She leaned forward, looking for Inge. "Can we go to your house and play with Silas later?"

"Not tonight, honey," Inge said. "Silas is home with his daddy. He's asleep." Inge rolled her eyes. "They probably both are."

"Why?" asked Zoe.

"Why? Because Uncle Bart is a little tired."

"What about Silas?"

"Silas is tired, too."

"Why?"

"Because he's a baby," Inge said. "Babies have to sleep a lot. That's how they grow. You slept all the time when you were a baby, too."

"Did not!" Zoe looked to Cara for support.

"All babies do," Cara said. "Do you want your crayons?"

"No!" Zoe began to pout. "Where's Mommy now?"

"She's backstage," Cara said.

"I love that," said Myra, a dreamy expression in her face. "Backstage! Makes it sound like you're dating some kind of rock bitch."

Cara frowned. "Are you calling my longtime partner a rock bitch?"

"Ugh," said Alice, "what is it with you people and that whole longtime partner lingo? It's so...submissive. It sounds as if you have a disease that requires permanent nursing. Why don't you come up with a better word?"

"There actually already is a better word," Myra said. "Wife."

"That's not altogether a bad idea," Alice said. "Why not simply get married?"

"Or at least move in together," Myra added.

Cara shook her head. "Actually," she said, "we're good. I'm sorry to disappoint you guys, but we're keeping things the way they are. Our arrangement is working just fine." She turned her attention back to Zoe. "So anyway," she said, "Mommy is going to sit on the stage. It will get really quiet and then Mommy will start reading from her book. Just the way she does at home. And when she's finished reading, the other lady is going to ask her many, many questions."

Zoe's eyes grew wide. "What kind of questions?"

"Questions about Mommy's book."

"Bunny!" The sound of her scream resounding through the auditorium made Zoe giggle, and she shouted again.

"That's fun, isn't it?" Cara said. "But you have to keep your voice down now, okay?" She put a finger to her lips. "Remember what we talked about?"

Zoe nodded and put a finger to her lips too. Her face became serious as she was reminded of her super-important tasks.

"They're not going to talk about Bunny," Cara told her. "They will another time, but this time they're talking about Mummy's other book."

Zoe looked at her blankly.

"The book that's called *What's Another Day*. Remember?"

"I want to play with Ede," Zoe declared, suddenly bored with being a grown-up.

Cara nodded. "Maybe tomorrow, okay? We'll ask Aunt Myra if we can take Ede to the park with us and have a little picnic."

"Sure," Myra said. "Take her. Take all of them!"

"Yay," whispered Zoe. She looked up at Cara, proud of herself for following the rules.

"Aw, honey." Cara put her arm around the girl and pulled her close. "You're doing that so well!"

Myra reached across Inge and tapped Cara on the knee. "I could even be persuaded to let you take Arend if you ask me real nice."

Cara shook her head. "Thanks. But no thanks. Our picnic's an all-girls party."

"Honey," said Myra, "your whole life is an all-girls party."

Slowly, the auditorium was filling up. It had wing access from both sides, and Cara turned her back to the stage to see two steady rows of teens walk down the steps and take their seats. It was funny, she mused, how Jude's audience seemed to have aged more than a decade in a little over a year. Gone were the sidekicks dressed as rabbits. Gone were the screaming toddlers, sitting cross-legged on the floor, listening breathlessly as Jude took them through another one of Bunny's adventures, their parents patiently waiting in the background. It was a very different crowd that she was catering to now—much more physically intimidating, often morose, shy and self-conscious, or inappropriately loud, insecure, doting, full of questions and criticism. Jude's novel had seemed to attract the more pensive ones among the young readers, the brooding types, the late night poets.

The idea for *What's Another Day* was born one night by accident, when Jude and Cara had been watching the sci-fi channel. Without realizing that the subject held any special interest to either of them, they started talking about time travel. Cara wondered what it would be like if you could hop back and forth in time, for the duration of your own life span, to consult your older self and base your choices on knowing what the outcome would be.

Before they knew it, Jude had produced the first draft—a wild ride of a teen time travel story. It took her a good many months to produce a final manuscript, but by then it was somehow clear to Jude, as well as to her agent, that this book stood a good chance of being a huge success. Jude, having been a pretty successful writer for years, realized that she hadn't known what true success was. She became a star, a Young Adult heroine.

"All I did," she'd say in many of the interviews that followed the publication, "was what I've always done—help kids come to terms with the scary mysteries of life in a way they will understand, whether they're four, or sixteen."

The teen readers became devotees. Jude was no stranger to admiration, but where the toddlers had loved Bunny, the teen fans were mostly interested in *her*, the writer.

There was the pressure of a sequel, naturally, but pressure came with the territory.

"Pressure schmessure," Cara said. "Sequel schmequel." Jude punched her, which was enough to take the pressure off. They had long since stopped being amazed at how often this was simply enough to resolve an issue—a stupid joke and a playful punch. It seemed that they had wanted the same things all along. The only things that were ever in the way were trust issues—assumptions about what they were convinced would go wrong, but, when put to the test, turned out not to go wrong at all. It helped that they were careful to avoid getting too symbiotic, and that they allowed each other the right of personal space and development. They were always there for each other, but as two separate beings, not as some kind of fused-together, double person. It was the kind of commitment they'd both been dreaming of, the kind that Cara had seen represented in the design of Jude's necklace on their very first date.

"They're all girls." Alice pouted as she watched the crowd begin to fill the rows of seats. "I told you this would happen. She could have doubled her audience if she hadn't insisted on going with that *thing*."

That thing was Alice's preferred reference to a crucial and gripping scene in the book, where the eighty-year-old protagonist tells her sixteen-year-old self that it's okay to be gay, and that yes, coming out of the closet now is essential to her future.

"We're actually very proud of that thing," said Cara.

Alice shrugged. "All I'm saying is that she's now a *lesbian* writer. It's a label she'll never get rid of. Ever."

"We're proud of the label too," Cara said.

"Personally, I love all the baby dykes." Inge was bouncing in her seat. "And the goths too."

"And all of them are in love with Jude," Myra said.

"What are goths about anyway?" Alice watched, with obvious fascination, a girl completely dressed in black with a face full of piercings sit down at the end of their row.

"What everybody is about at that age," Myra said. "Angst."

"So why weren't they around when we were young? We had angst!"

"They were." Cara smiled. "They just didn't get out much."

In less than half an hour, the auditorium was packed—all two hundred and fifty seats filled. The stage was complete now, with two leather armchairs, a large potted palm and a table full of water bottles and glasses between them.

"When is the movie starting?" Zoe asked. She was pointing to the automated screen at the back of the stage. A lightshow was projected on it now that may or may not be actual footage of the aurora borealis.

"There's not going to be a movie," Cara told Zoe. "Or maybe just a very short one, with Mommy in it."

"Mommy's not in the movie!" Zoe shook her head at so much ignorance.

"But she sure is a star," Alice said.

Zoe, not particularly fond of Alice, stuck out her tongue to her.

When the lights were dimmed, Cara felt the anxiety she always did the moment any interview started. It was worse now—she didn't think Jude had ever talked in front of so many people before. Sometimes, exactly at moments like this, Cara would think back, longingly, to Jude's Bunny days—when it had all, in spite of her initial fear of the little ones, been so simple, so low-key. Cara was in awe of the ease with which Jude seemed to have made the transition to having such a different position to her readers. And not just to her readers, either. She had a different position as a writer too—it was almost as if she were held more accountable, as if what she had to say mattered far more than it used to. Cara, very much part of the writer's life, but still a bystander, had adapted to the changes more slowly, and never quite as convincingly. She would compare the change to moving from the countryside to a large city—it was much louder and busier, and much more stressful. On the other hand, the rewards were considerable.

Cara was so immersed in her thoughts that it was the applause that made her realize Jude was walking onto the stage. Cara could actually see her slip into her role. She wasn't adopting a different persona—she was always Jude, even in public, but with more of a sharp edge. She sat up straighter, talked a little fancier, smiled a little more, and she was endlessly more patient, answering questions she had been asked a hundred times before as if this was actually the first time she heard them.

It was always somewhat of a mystery to Cara how she related to Jude when she was doing things in an official writer capacity. Cara was her life partner, but there was a layer of something impenetrable that stuck to her on occasions like these, almost as if she were wearing some sort of costume. She smiled. Costumes seemed to play an important role in their lives—Santa, Bunny, and now the invisible costume of the idol.

Jude took a sip of water as the interviewer cleared her throat and fired her first question at her. Jude smiled and put down her glass.

"A muse, I guess." she said. "At least for me. Any good story starts with my muse whispering something in my ear. From that moment on, it's simply hard work. It's simply a matter of sitting down and getting the job done."

She sat up straighter. Cara smiled, knowing that Jude was going to shine. And although she loved seeing Jude so confident, and so successful, she couldn't help thinking that three hours from now they would be home, put Zoe to bed, and just sit in the dark with a glass of wine, very close together.

Those hours, when all the costumes had come off, would always be her favorite.

About Hazel Yeats

Hazel Yeats resides in the Netherlands, the country of flat polders, green pastures, and lots of water. She knew from an early age that she wanted to write, but it wasn't until decades later that she finally wrote a novel. Once she had, there was no going back—she was hooked.

When she's not slaving away at her day job, she's cycling, sipping cappuccinos, or getting her hands dirty by growing her own veggies. And she sings, in a very unambitious choir. You wouldn't peg her for a soprano, but she is.

CONNECT WITH HAZEL YEATS:
E-Mail: hazelyeats@outlook.com

Other Books from Ylva Publishing

www.ylva-publishing.com

Never-Tied Nora
(Girl Meets Girl Series – Book #1)

Cheyenne Blue

ISBN: 978-3-95533-451-2
Length: 131 pages (38,000 words)

Nora Kelly's London Irish family have only one rule when it comes to dating: Nora can date any woman she wants—as long as she's not a Flannery. The Kellys and the Flannerys have been feuding for generations, and time has not lessened the hatred.

But footloose Nora has just met the woman of her dreams, and suddenly commitment isn't a dirty word. Trouble is, Geraldine is a Flannery.

All the Little Moments

G Benson

ISBN: 978-3-95533-341-6
Length: 350 pages (132,000 words)

Anna is focused on her career as an anaesthetist. When a tragic accident leaves her responsible for her young niece and nephew, her life changes abruptly. Completely overwhelmed, Anna barely has time to brush her teeth in the morning let alone date a woman. But then she collides with a long-legged stranger.

Once

L.T. Smith

ISBN: 978-3-95533-399-7
Length: 295 pages (77,000 words)

Beth Chambers' life is no fairytale. After four years in a destructive relationship, Beth decides enough is enough and leaves her girlfriend, taking Dudley, her dog, with her. At her lowest point, she meets Amy Fletcher, a woman who appears to have it all—and whom she believes would never want more than friendship. Beth needs to believe in magic once more for her dreams to come true. But can she?

Mac vs. PC

Fletcher DeLancey

ISBN: 978-3-95533-187-0
Length: 148 pages (32,000 words)

Computer tech Anna Petrowski is used to people assuming her advice is free, even on weekends. Elizabeth Markel catches her eye precisely because she needs that advice, but doesn't ask. It's the beginning of something special...except Elizabeth is not what Anna thinks.

People and computers have one thing in common: they're both capable of self-sabotage. But computers are easier to fix.

Coming from Ylva Publishing

www.ylva-publishing.com

Rewriting the Ending

hp tune

A chance meeting in an airport lounge and a shared flight itinerary leaves Juliet and Mia connected. But how do you stay connected when you've only known each other for twenty four hours, are destined for different continents and each have a past to reconcile?

Where the Light Plays

C. Fonseca

Dr. Caitlin Quinn is a sophisticated, self-assured Irish art historian visiting Australia on sabbatical. That doesn't mean she can't enjoy the local scenery – especially sun kissed Surfcoast artist, Andi Rey. Their attraction is unstoppable, but their lives are moving in opposite directions. Andi doesn't need distractions and a woman that eschews commitment spells trouble, with a capital "T".

Bunny Finds a Friend
© 2016 by Hazel Yeats

ISBN: 978-3-95533-499-4

Also available as e-book.

Published by Ylva Publishing, legal entity of Ylva Verlag, e.Kfr.

Ylva Verlag, e.Kfr.
Owner: Astrid Ohletz
Am Kirschgarten 2
65830 Kriftel
Germany

www.ylva-publishing.com

First edition: 2016

Credits
Edited by Gill McKnight
Cover Design & Print Layout by Streetlight Graphics

15206747R00131

Printed in Great Britain
by Amazon.co.uk, Ltd.,
Marston Gate.